FLORENTINE
FINISH

Other titles in the Allison & Busby American Crime series

Cornelius
Hirschberg

FLORENTINE
FINISH

Allison & Busby
Published by W. H. Allen & Co. Plc

An Allison & Busby book
Published in 1989 by
W. H. Allen & Co. Plc
Sekforde House, 175/9 St. John Street,
London, EC1V 4LL

Printed in Great Britain by
Cox & Wyman Ltd, Reading, Berks

ISBN 0 85031 850 5

I

I don't bother with deals off the job – private deals they're called – as a general rule. I must be the only man in the business who doesn't. But I had never had a chance before to make such a fat dollar. That's why I was standing that Monday in Moselle's Exchange and at Barney Moselle's own section of it.

It's a scene, the exchange, especially at noon, if you care for scenes: a sultan's palace remodeled into a farmers' market, with emeralds for turnips and jewelry counters for vegetable stalls.

I was used to it. My eye was on the little item in front of me: a tapered half-inch of winking ice, a concentrated sparkle of ancient hell-fire, lying in a slick white folding paper on the counter.

"Mr. Moselle," I said, "Barney – it's a sale in a thousand. This guy has the money. He knows me from way back and he'll take what I give him, but it has to stand up. The A.P. must be right."

Moselle was mild and considerate as he always is. He's the only distinguished-looking man I've ever been able to like.

"Saul," he said, "I get the idea, I want you to make your sale. There's nothing for me in letting the merchandise go out and come back. I'm giving you the right price. If you don't take too much profit, this diamond will stand up in any legitimate appraisal."

"How do I get a legitimate A.P.?"

"Sell it on the understanding that the appraisal must be in writing. I'll back you up. If the appraisal isn't good, I'll talk to your customer myself, and if that doesn't do it, I'll

1

give them my valuation on my letter head. They can take it to anybody in the world."

It was fair enough. Moselle was too big a name to breeze off, and if Barney would go that far, the price had to be O.K. I studied the centimeter of pear-shaped crystal smiling between us. It looked very, very good, clear as rain water, and I'd swear I could see the blue. I know diamonds, though not like Moselle; few men do. I couldn't go wrong on it.

I asked: "Can I keep it until Thursday?"

Barney nodded and motioned to his clerk. "Write it up, Henry"

Henry got out the memorandum book and started scribbling, but he carefully specified the weight, 5.21 carats. He shoved the book at me. I signed somewhere in the middle of the page – I can't stand those guys who work their names into the line next to the merchandise entry, as if a man who would trust you with 5.21 carats at $2,660 per carat would write in something over your signature – I hate people who see things that way.

Henry, however (his last name was Henry), carefully drew lines under the figure $13,858.60, to show that there was only one item on the consignment. Henry knows his business and he's a very polite fellow.

"Thanks, Barney," I called out as Henry gave me my envelope. Moselle raised one hand; he was leaning over another counter opposite a thin Israeli in beard and skullcap, and a paper full of carat sizes lay between them. The Israeli probably had sixty carats strapped on him somewhere; I saw no sample case.

The exchange was working as I walked to the door, fifty booths gladly rented by Moselle to anybody who wanted to compete with him. There was ten million dollars' worth of jewelry in the place, and they were buying it as if it were hamburgers. It's only one of a dozen exchanges on that block; anybody with a pocket full of diamonds or pearls can lease a counter and be in business.

The sun came down clear and strong on seething Forty-seventh Street. The block – Fifth to Sixth Avenue – was packed. Gesticulating jewelry men: casters, polishers, jewelers, engine turners, diamond cutters, diamond polishers, setters, engravers, ring carvers, watchmakers, casemakers, modelmakers, factory owners, clerks – all these jammed into two sidewalks of one block: all the people who work in the innumerable lofts and offices overhead; by the hundreds, the thousands, out for a quick bite of lunch. And the salesmen: strained and eager; tired, always tired; each man looking for his corned beef on rye, his pastrami on an onion roll, his coffee, his beer, his celery tonic; some with sample cases, some dragging those little carts – that infinity of little handcarts with their treasures of gold, platinum, pearls, diamonds. And most of the cart pushers with ulcers.

The nationalities were Puerto Rican, Italian, Jew, Levantine, and an occasional Irishman – probably a pawnbroker or a pawnbroker's man. And the oddballs, the ones who would be the straight characters anywhere else, those peculiar Americans, the Forty-seventh Street customers.

My own store, the one I worked in, was only two doors east, but I went the other way, crossed Sixth Avenue, and entered the White Lily bar on the west side of the avenue – the Avenue of the Americas. The dark, air-conditioned dankness felt good, and I found the kind of table I wanted. Those places have certain tables reserved for waitress service and other tables where you can eat your meal after you serve yourself. The meats are in front as you go in, slabs of beef, ham, etc., and maybe a couple of cooked dishes. The long, old-fashioned bar runs opposite.

The trick is to sit at a table not reserved for service and then accept service. If you tip five cents more than usual, you can own the joint, because you're not occupying one of the waitresses' tables; on the contrary, you are forcing some self-service cheapie to accept service in order to get a seat, That way I could sit and rest my feet for three quarters of an hour.

This time I couldn't. I was due back in twenty minutes. I called the waitress and took my usual – a brisket on rye, cole slaw, and a stein of beer, When she brought them, I asked:

"Rose, who is that dark man two booths ahead?"

3

Rose turned casually (she's been serving me for two years, and I've had a lot of her confidences).

"Never saw him before."

He was big, no jewelry man for sure, and he looked tough. I hadn't seen him around; he was either a hood or a cop, but I couldn't place him. He looked too prosperous for the White Lily; moreover, I was positive he had a gun. I'm not so blasé as I thought, I said to myself; if I didn't have Moselle's diamond on me, I'd never have noticed that character.

"Saul," Rose said to me sadly, "I haven't heard from him."

"It doesn't look good," I told her (she had fallen for some fellow who had told her he lived in Queens, and it wasn't working out). "I have to make a quick getaway this time." I laid one dollar and twenty-five cents on the table, which gave her a quarter tip, and got up to her usual earnest thank you – I had my own troubles. She was over thirty, had half-raised a daughter, and should have known how to protect herself, but it doesn't seem to work that way for a lot of people.

I caught the big guy's eye as I went past him, which was exactly what I didn't want, and shows how imagination can throw you off. I reflected that, although I could see the bulge of his gun, he couldn't see the bulge of my diamond.

II

It was Monday and the store was busy. I put Moselle's diamond in the safe, went behind the counters and took the nearest customer. He was a slow starter, so I began another until Number 1 woke up. Number 2 only wanted to brood over watch straps; I dropped him and found two regulars from Sophisticated Rings who use quite a bit of goods.

They asked for ordinary engraved gold wedding rings. Naturally, everything I had was too high, even though we work on very small markup. But Dominic finally took three rings and two sterling I.D. bracelets. His pal, Torres, wanted a diamond engagement ring, about a carat, platinum, Tiffany setting, with baguettes.

"How much, Joe?" I asked.

"Not over two hundred."

I have more patience with the Puerto Ricans than with anybody else because they're so damn polite.

"Joe," I said, "I think maybe your customer wants a zircon, I have a special zircon for you; it's a zircon with a genuine carbon spot." This is very funny because only diamonds can have carbon spots – I'm a great comedian with the customers.

In the end I found him a three-quarter carat in white gold for $250.

"Imperfect?" Joe asks me.

"Guaranteed. Tell your customer anybody says it's perfect can have his money back."

I got out the memo book and wrote up the two of them. By this time the character for the watch strap had reached a decision. I rang up his 50 cents, and started to put the strap on his battered watch – crazy as it sounds, we give that service. Inevitably his pushpins were no good, so I had to leave the counter and go over to the watchmaker's bench to select the right pin.

We don't have too much space for such a busy store; no chairs, mirrors, or anything like that. It's set up for fast operation – in and out. At that moment we had four men behind the counters, including the two bosses. The first pin I tried went flying through space, and when I looked up to see whose eye I had put out, I spotted the tough man from the beer joint coming through the door.

The Holmes Electric burglar alarm runs under the counters and along the pillar by the watchmaker's desk. It goes to show what imagination can do to you; when I saw that face, I saw the café, I saw Rose, I saw his gun and my diamond, and, so help me, I grabbed that alarm and almost squeezed it. Within three minutes the cops would have come in shooting, but just in time I heard my name. The man had asked Jake Corbin if he could see me.

I came out of it and said, "I'm Saul Handy."

He smiled, tough but friendly. "I'm Al Light. Ed Bender said you would give me a good buy on a watch. You're seeing Ed tonight?"

"I was figuring to get to his place by 7:30," I answered reluctantly. I didn't like Mr. Light to know where I was going with Moselle's stone.

"He's expecting you," he said.

I got down to business and sold him a Longines *Admiral*. He wanted a heavy-duty piece and his taste was conservative. (Strictly speaking, since Ed Bender had sent him to me, he was my customer, but I have a deal with the Corbins to split the profit on my own trade. That way I don't have the headaches.) I set the Longines, put it on his wrist, and thanked him. He said good-by – he wasn't a loose talker. I had given him fifty off list, which was probably better than he could have done anywhere else.

He bothered me. I had been a cop once, although I don't look it; I made detective on the Chicago police just before the Korean War, but I wanted to be a soldier and after I came out of the army I never went back to police work. My father had owned a pretty nice jewelry store in Springfield, Illinois, and although everything went in the liquidation after his death, I *was* born in the business and somehow I was back in it. But you can't be a cop for nothing; this Al Light seemed to me like a lot of people I had come across in Chicago.

The day stumbled to its end. I found gold charms for meandering dowagers, supplied miscellaneous merchandise to assorted factory workers who wanted to be businessmen, and sold a baguette wedding ring in platinum, fairly clean stuff, to a young couple sent to us by a man with a small engine-turning business down on Canal Street.

Then I put the stock into the safes, put Moselle's diamond in my pocket, waited till Murray Corbin got the all-clear signal from Holmes Electric, and called it a day. It was six-thirteen. The last customer, and the one who stuck me, as usual, was Abe Berkowitz, a modelmaker from V.F. Berman's, who thought he was cut out to be a salesman.

I had my Olds in the parking lot on the next block. I got it into the traffic and set out for Bender's residence.

Oddly enough, as I came out of the yard, I saw Light walking in. He must have had his car in the lot. He saw me too; he brought his hand up to his big, tough face.

III

Bender's home was Crestmere, a part of Westchester with no welfare problem at all. He evidently made a lot of money, since neither he nor his family had any when I knew them in Springfield and he had it now. I didn't know what he did, but I had heard he was some kind of broker. Insurance maybe.

It was way past seven by the time I found the place. I hadn't eaten. I was nervous over the sale and, along with that, tired and droopy. The property showed big in my headlights with the house set half an acre behind the side-walk. It had two stories, a bank of garages, and landscape gardening. I turned into the driveway and pulled up at the side entrance.

I half expected a synthetic English butler to open up for me, but Bender was at the door by the time I reached it. He led me into a large brown leather library. The bar showed more use than the books, which is all right too.

"What will you have, Saul – bourbon?"

"Please," I answered, and I collapsed into a brown club chair that looked broken in. The lamps were soft, the chair was softer, and I knew how tired I was when the liquor hit me. Bender sat watching me enjoy my drink, and he had another ready when I had finished. I like two straight before I take any water. He remembered that from the army; we had gone in from Springfield together. We never had been pals, but neither of us liked to drink alone. That was all I really knew about him, except for schooldays. His father had been a plumber.

"Mr. Light bought a watch from me today," I remarked. "Thanks for sending him."

"He told me."

"A business associate?"

"He works for me."

What the hell doing? I thought. Light was no customers' man, unless you have strange customers. Bender didn't look that way at all; he was tall with small bones and a face mostly profile but handsome. He looked like an actor. He had plenty of nerve, though; I had seen that.

The room was decorated with several pictures of horses, in color and expensively framed, all very masculine. But one, a painting, maybe two feet by three, seemed off pitch. It was a scrambled affair, red and brown, vaguely suggesting a big slab of meat twisted around an invisible barber pole. I blinked and Bender noticed it.

"Like my art, Saul?" His grin was off center, like the meat.

"What is it?"

"That's a horse. Couldn't put a cow in here."

"It seems ready for the glue factory."

"You're way off. He's running. Running round a bend in the track."

"So. Must be an acquired taste. When did you learn to like such things?"

"A gift from my wife. The wall needed a picture. Helene really goes in for that stuff."

I pulled my eyes off the mishmash. "He's sure trying; he's run his skin off."

He laughed harshly – he always had a rough laugh. "I'd put ten on his nose, but I can't find it."

I finished my drink.

"Want to look at something fine, Ed?"

He nodded. I took out the envelope and opened the paper on the cocktail table.

"It'll show more fire if you use stronger light," I said, but that was just to say something; the naked little beauty was blazing in that shining white paper like a spot of flame. And somehow it looked enormous.

Bender picked up the paper carefully and peered into the diamond. "Funny how they're going for these pear-shapes now," he remarked.

9

"They have more life than emerald-cuts."

"How big is it?"

"Five carats and a quarter. Five-twenty-one on the scales."

"Perfect?"

"Absolutely."

"No flaws?"

"There are no flaws. What's more important, it's a stone of elegant color and fire. They don't cut them better either. It's cut like a drawing of a diamond in a book."

"How much?"

I took out a bit of paper I had figured on. "It will cost me $13,858. Add 5 per cent commission and 10 per cent federal tax on top of that, and its comes to $15,937–" It was the highest price I had ever quoted.

"Ten per cent federal tax?"

"It's got to be, Ed. It's too big a stone to take chances on. My supplier has my name and resale number down in black and white."

He studied me. He was through looking at the stone. Then he went to a desk set at right angles to the fireplace and picked up a phone. "Can you come into the library for a few minutes, Helene? I want you to look at something." To me he said, "It's no surprise to her. She's had it coming for a long time and she knows I'm working on it."

A tall and sumptuous woman came into the room: under thirty, blond, with the carriage of a dancer, and the kind of eyes that people have only when they never need to ask twice for things – her father was no plumber.

"Helene, this is Saul Handy. He's brought us something." He pointed at the paper.

She held out her hand. "Ed has often told me about you, Mr. Handy." Which would have been surprising if true, since we had seen each other only three times in the last eight years. Then she looked at the diamond, and I seemed to see the flash of that fiery icicle come back out of her dark-blue eyes. She looked at it quietly for a moment and said, "It's beautiful."

"Shall I buy it, Helene?"

"If you want me to have it."

He turned to me. "You're sure, Saul, that's the right price?"

I took my eyes off that woman, took out my copy of Moselle's memo, and offered it to him. "See for yourself."

His hand didn't move. "What's that?"

"My bill."

"Keep it. Leave the stone and I'll send you a check."

I put the memo in my pocket. "There's only one thing, Ed. I have the diamond on consignment. I don't own it. I must return it or pay for it by Thursday, and I don't have that kind of money."

His eyes were on mine. "Do you want cash?"

"Now? That much? Here?"

He went over to the wall, swept the crazy picture aside, and exposed a wall safe. It opened quickly enough, and in another moment he had counted down fifteen thousand-dollar bills off a much larger bundle. Nine paltry hundreds, two twenties, and I had my money. I solemnly took three singles out of my pocket and gave the man his change. I had exactly twenty-two more in my wallet. I smiled, a little shamefaced. "I'm used to carrying precious merchandise, but not cash. I see familiarity breeds contempt in everything."

He laughed shortly; she smiled at me with overpowering graciousness. I reflected that no amount of familiarity could ever breed contempt toward a woman like that. But what kind of broker keeps that much cash on hand?

I placed those thousand-dollar bills carefully inside my coat pocket. "Do you want me to handle the setting?" I asked.

"Probably. I'll let you know this week."

This meant he was going to have it appraised. "I would advise a three-prong, handmade mounting. Nothing added to it – you can't dress up that diamond. Thanks a lot, Ed." I turned to his wife. "You'll love it, Mrs. Bender. You'll appreciate it more as your eye becomes used to it. It really is a stone in a thousand."

"I'm sure it is, Mr. Handy. I'm very grateful to you for the trouble I know you've gone to."

Her perfume was regal; I blacked out as if I had been presented at court. What you can have if you have what it takes!

IV

I couldn't get out of the store until two o'clock the next day, but tired and hungry as I was, I went straight to Moselle's Exchange. Moselle was standing in his usual corner. I handed him fourteen of Bender's thousand-dollar bills and with perfect nonchalance waited for my change.

"A hundred, Saul?" He also was a good nonchalance man.

"Make it twenties, Barney, if it's not inconvenient."

He nodded, went to the counter safe, brought out a roll of bills and put them in the cash drawer. Then he counted out seven twenties, added the chicken feed, put the thousands back into the safe, and said: Nice sale. Did you make anything?"

"Five per cent. I was afraid to skip the federal."

He looked surprised. "Maybe it's better," he added thoughtfully. "You might sleep better. How about the city sales?"

"I sold it in Westchester."

"Well, you didn't make too much, but it's a sure sale anyhow."

I grinned. "I can take car depreciation off my income tax. It was a nice diamond."

"The cutting is book-perfect. I never saw a big stone hit the theoretical proportions closer."

I had thought it was rather a fine-cut myself, but my experience is a waste of time when you have a man like Moselle. If he says it's regular cut, it's regular.

"Hope you have more of them," he added. He took my memo out of his file and held it out to me. I tore it to pieces and gave him the scraps. He dropped them into a wastebasket – all exactly as it goes when I'm behind the counter, only I don't get them so big – not by some $13,000.

A memo is the last remainder, in law, of recourse against the body of the debtor. You don't buy on memo; you borrow merchandise under a time limit, and the owner of the goods can slap you in jail unless you either return his property or pay up on demand. An immense number of jewelry transactions are handled that way. For one thing, it's proof against bankruptcy

I said good-by, waved to Henry, and began to push through the crowds in the exchange. As I did so I noticed an exquisite brunette standing inside Moselle's section (his is the largest on the floor). It was probably his wife; I had never seen her before. She was rather small, slender, dressed to perfection, and finished like an emerald-cut. She was a lot younger than Moselle. Distinction was all over her. She was what jewelry ads try to make their models look like. I didn't notice any jewelry on her from where I stood; if she felt the need for a few pieces, she wouldn't have to go far.

So I had three things on my mind as I headed for the White Lily. Why did Bender keep so much cash in the house? What did Mr. Al Light do for him? What do you have to do to get women like Mrs. Bender and Mrs. Moselle? – None of it was any business of mine.

Rose looked awful as she mopped up my table. Her tables haven't been ready to eat from since she met that vanishing Indian from Queens.

"How do you know he's not married with three children?" I asked her.

She stared at me as if my face was falling off. "He told me he was divorced."

I nodded. If I didn't do something to break the mood, she'd be putting cucumber salad in my second beer, so I said:

"Find out anything about that hard character was here yesterday?"

"I think he's got something to do with the numbers." she said. "He talked to several men yesterday and one of them has written a few numbers for me."

"That's what you need – the numbers. Christ, Rose, you are an awful sucker." If Bender was in the policy racket, then Rose had put her mite into my $693 profit. Rose was a pretty woman with plenty of figure.

I finished my London broil on rye and gave her $1.45. Again I hadn't had enough time to sit off my feet.

Then she said, "Could you recommend a private detective?"

"What for?"

"Weren't you a policeman once?"

"In Chicago. There are no more private detectives in New York – only investigators."

"That's all I need."

I saw where she was heading if you could call it heading. "Rose, lay off. I don't know any private investigators, and if I did I wouldn't tell you. Either the guy will or he won't. What do you want to do – blackmail him?"

She turned her eyes into mine – I was standing – and I swear they don't put it over so good on TV. "I don't know what I want to do," she said.

I couldn't help but feel sorry for her; she's such a schmuck. She'd worked within five blocks of Times Square and half a block from Forty-seventh Street for six years, and she hadn't learned a thing.

Forty-seventh Street's a funny place. It has more wise guys per square foot than any other street on earth. A circus or a carnival is peanuts to it. You start at Fifth Avenue, drifting past Brentano's and the Longines-Wittnauer Building, and you veer gently to west. In ten feet you have left Fifth Avenue so far behind you might as well be in a Tangier bazaar. Each number on the street is famous for whatever the jewelry business is famous for. At Number 8, opposite the Longines Building, you hit the first big exchange. Number 15 is the Diamond Club, where nobody gets in without a member as chaperon and without ninety carats strapped to his navel. Each number means something distinct to all the thousands of boys in the know. The entire street is lined with gold and precious stones, blazing at you from a solid block of eye-level, shatterproof window glass. Millions of dollars' worth of gems hang

15

burning in the air and tens of millions more smolder in the rear.

Naturally the Jews have a lot to do with Forty-seventh Street. Jewelry has always been a Jewish business, and where there are Jews there's life; an intense life, furious and worked on close margin. The boys say you don't need much Yiddish to be understood on Forty-seventh Street; just two words – "gelt" and "schmuck": If you have no gelt, you're a schmuck. Still, they all seem a little sad to me; they're all like Rose if you look close. So am I.

The rest of the afternoon was fast and tedious. I do get tired sometimes explaining the same things over and over again. . . . "Very few genuine star sapphires are sold since the Lindes came out. They are real star sapphires, but made by man; there's nothing simulated about them. The stone is chemically identical with a mined stone. No, these are not Germans; our rings are genuine Lindes. . . . We carry Numbers 4, 6, 8, 10 chains. You can't see the difference when you look at the in-between numbers. Eighteen or twenty-four inches. I'll shorten a twenty-four if you want twenty-two. How much does two inches of number six chain cost you? Use it for a safety some time. . . . We can't get pierced charms back faster. It will be ready Friday. . . . The birthstone for November is a topaz, but it won't show up on a charm. O.K. if you say so. . . . Get me the exact model watch, the retail, etc., and I'll try to get it for you. That's a case number you've got. It doesn't tell me a thing. I need a model number or name. *Admiral, Lord Clancy, Lady Schmaltz, La Petite Feet* . . ."

And the telephone! It's no joke to handle two customers at one time, watch your gold, and keep picking up the phone. "No, we don't keep open evenings, God forbid. We are closed every Saturday. *Murray, is Sandborg's bracelet back? It's being lengthened* . . . What's the repair number? We can't search through two hundred watches. Certainly it's guaranteed; by all means bring it back if anything goes wrong. There'll be a charge, but bring it back. . . . At these prices? Only the smile is free. . . . Go to a materials house; we don't have silver spring rings. . . . That size pearl runs about seventy to the mome. . . . Graduated? Six and one-half millimeters from twenty dollars, knotted. . . . They're one-piece rings; I can stretch them."

It came to an end and I put the goods away. Amateurs never stop marveling that the entire stock of a jewelry store is put in the safe every night and taken out every morning, although it's been done since the time of Ali Baba. Bright thinkers try to devise (across the counter) something which will either do it mechanically or do away with the need for it, but their ideas are always a hundred times more expensive than our backs.

The Holmes gave its signal and I went out. It was cooler and getting dark. I was tired and jumpy, but still feeling pretty good; not so much because I had made $700 but because I had enjoyed laying those fourteen thousand-dollar bills on Moselle's counter. I had nothing to do. I'm a bachelor. I wasn't hungry, so I went to the Chien Lung and had the $2.75 dinner with spareibs. And then I walked around to my hotel and looked at TV for an hour. There was a thriller in which the police were looking for where the cyanide came from that killed the jeweler's wife. Since every jewelry business has cyanide on the premises, I lost interest and went to bed.

V

The next morning began like all the rest. A skin diver came in to pick up a Zodiak skin diver's watch, and Murray Corbin and I tried diving for her skin, but she swam out of reach and went down to wherever she had come up from. The noon rush began, and I must have written up twenty memos in two hours – that's besides checking for returns on memos outstanding and seeing that I get paid for whatever they keep.

"Can I have a stein right away?" I asked Rose, when I finally collapsed into a booth and kicked off my shoes. For once she went along with the idea and I had finished the stein by the time she brought me my corned beef on rye.

Rose sat down opposite me. It was 2:30; the place was almost empty. Beer affects me on an empty stomach and I felt the weariness fall away. Rose began to look prettier; in the mood she was in she would have been a pushover, but somehow a brother-sister business had crept in and it wasn't for me.

"I don't understand," she told me. "I would have sworn he wasn't that kind. He's a gentleman, you know – I guess I should have gone to bed with him."

I eased up on my chewing long enough to say, "You can't tell, Rose. Sometimes that works and sometimes it doesn't. You were there and you played it as you saw it. I was inclined to think that you should have given him something. Then he would have had something to lose. But the chances are it wouldn't have made any difference. You built too many castles."

She said, "Once we went to a hotel. I couldn't bring him up to my apartment – I never do that – so he said, 'Why

18

don't we go to a hotel and play cards or something?' So I excused myself for a minute and ran into a cigar store and bought a pack of cards. When we got to the hotel. I said, 'Do you have cards?' He looked at me. I took out the pack. So we played cards. What worries me is that after a while we were both lying in bed, dressed, alongside each other. That's all it was. We just lay in bed, but don't you think if a man *really* cares for a woman he can't lie against her that way and not have an orgasm?"

Rose is by no means an ignorant girl as you can see by that word "orgasm." But I am rather ignorant about such delicate issues as she was raising. I ran details of my own experience through my mind and said:

"Not necessarily."

She got up, necessarily but reluctantly, to give some attention to a man who had been trying to get some for twenty minutes. "Wouldn't you see if you can find him?"

That thrilled me.

"I'd be glad to pay you," she went on.

"And that could put me in jail. You need a license before you take money for tracking down men who don't want to get married." I had an Illinois license which I had never used, but I wasn't telling her.

I thought of Ed Bender's appraisal as I walked back to work. Appraisals are funny things; anybody with a letter-head can make appraisals; I do it myself, using the firm's stationery. There is an animal called a licensed appraiser, whatever that means, but he's needed only for certain legal work. All in all, it's the loosest business since they closed down the red-light district. Depending on where Bender took my diamond, he could get appraisals for any amounts beween $5,000 and $30,000. If he went to a cheap operator, the punk would try to kill my sale so he could make one himself, and the appraisal would be rotten. If he went to a high-class store where they charge plenty for their own stuff and wouldn't dare value mine at less, the appraisal might be wonderful. I had friends in the racket, including a well-known pawnbroker, who would have been glad to take care of my interests for a small private fee, but if Bender had wanted me to recommend an appraiser he would have asked me.I hoped he would go to one of the big department stores. He wouldn't be satisfied for less than $5,000 over the price he had paid.

The store was empty when I got back except for the Corbins and two men. Before I could take off my jacket (we work in shirt sleeves) Jake Corbin said:

"These gentlemen wish to see you."

They were big, flushed, baggy, heavy-footed, and all cop. I asked, "What can I do for you?"

"You're Saul Handy?"

I agreed.

"We would like you to come down to headquarters and look at something."

"Is anybody hurt?" (Not that I have any relations in New York.)

"Oh, no. We want you to look at a diamond."

I said to the Corbins, "One of ours?"

Jake answered, "I don't know a thing about it."

"Must I go now? Won't it keep until we close?"

"No. We're sorry."

They didn't look it. I looked at the bosses again. They looked blank. The detectives looked blank. I began to feel blank. We went out together.

VI

They didn't offer information on the way downtown, and I didn't ask. Their names were Druckman and Bramson. Bramson wanted to know what I could do for him on an Omega Seamaster. Druckman didn't want anything.

They have a big place downtown. I should have felt at home in a police station and police headquarters, but I can't say I did, After going through the usual corridors, we went into the usual hideous chamber. It was nicely filled by a policeman in uniform, another in plain clothes, Al Light and Ed Bender. I stood looking from one to the other. The man in uniform went out. The plain-clothes man said, "I'm Lieutenant Marder. Sit down."

I sat down. Bender looked at my face. Light looked at my face. I didn't feel good. The lieutenant said, "Can you identify this?" and I didn't need to look at it to know what I was to identify. The pear-shape lay in the same paper and it loomed as big as a tidal wave.

I said, in the general direction of Bender, "It's the same stone, isn't it?"

"I'll ask the questions," Marder said. "Just tell me whether you can identify it."

"Do you have a glass?" I asked, feeling very stupid.

Marder pushed a loupe at me. It was a good one, Bausch and Lomb, ten-x, and entirely professional. And he handed me a diamond tweezers.

I'm not too graceful at best with loose stones. I've never handled them in big quantities like the guys who do nothing else. It was all I could do to steady my hand and pick it up. I took my time examining it, because I couldn't think.

I couldn't think at all. I did reflect that these must be boys from the jewelry detail, if they have one in New York.

The diamond was as clear, as fine, as beautiful, as it had been on Moselle's counter. I said, "I presume this is the diamond I sold Mr. Bender, because there is no other reason for us to be here. If you want an absolute identification, you will have to ask Barney Moselle. I only had the stone in my possession for maybe six hours and I didn't study it. Anyway, I couldn't put my knowledge of diamonds against an expert like Moselle – it certainly looks good enough to be the same one."

Marder asked, "Do you have a bill from Moselle?"

"No. I took it out on consignment and when I paid for it I tore up the memo."

Druckman asked, "Did you pay the federal tax?"

I didn't like his tone. "It's not due," I answered, as snappy as I could.

"Nor the city sales tax either?"

I began to get annoyed. "We citizens pay our taxes when the law requires it. We don't fly down to the district director every time we write a sale."

Marder said, "If you had paid the tax you might have a receipt for that."

I studied him a little. He was of average size, like me, and didn't look particularly like a policeman. He was sharp featured, dark haired, and had a cleft chin. I would have accepted him for a jewelry man.

I said, "Mr. Moselle will acknowledge receipt of the money – what's all this about?"

Then Bender spoke, "Do you see any flaws in it?"

That got me. "Impossible," I snapped, and I caught the stone in the tweezers again and really began to look into it. It was as clear as anything that ever came out of the ground. I again noticed that the girdle, which is the edge all around a diamond where the prongs take hold when it is set, was rather sharply cut, more like a so-called fine-cut. I said firmly:

"There are no flaws in this diamond visible with a ten-power loupe," A ten-power glass is standard.

22

Marder pulled out a drawer of his desk and took out another glass. "Try a twenty," he said.

The sweat came out. "Where?" I asked. Something *had* to be some place.

"Almost at the culet. Try looking right down through the table."

A twenty-x has a poor spread becauses the focal point is necessarily short. A five-carat stone can be examined with it only one portion at a time. I shifted the tweezers up and down, very conscious that Marder was sneering at my clumsy technique; and then I caught it, a tiny bubble, like a bubble of air in a glass of water, almost at the point of the diamond. I could have found it with the ten-power, if I had had any reason for looking for it. I set the tweezers and its precious freight down, took a breath, and relaxed a little.

"The bubble?"

Marder nodded.

"It's still worth the money, every cent of it. I think it's even a finer stone than I had realized. It's the best diamond I've ever seen. But how did the police get in on it?"

Druckman spoke from behind me. "You think it's worth the money?"

"Yes, I do." I turned sidewise. "I don't get the whole act, Bender. I sold it for perfect. It was warranted perfect to me by one of the largest and most respected diamond dealers in this country. I'm not sure that it still wouldn't stand up as perfect in a court of law. But I gave my word you could have your money back if you wanted it, and that's the way it stands. It's a splendid buy. You'll never do better but you can have your cash. Did you have it appraised?"

Bender turned up an eye like a flounder. "Al, the man wants to know if you had it appraised."

Light's face was savage. "I had it appraised."

I asked, "What did you get?"

Light got up. "The cops. That's what I got. The cops."

I used to be a policeman and I still don't like certain types getting tough with me.

"Maybe," I said, "the appraiser is allergic to thugs. Did

you go in with your rod in your hand?" And ignoring the suffusion of red that spread from Light's neck to his hair, I turned to Marder.

"Lieutenant, would you mind briefing me why I'm here, why Mr. Bender and his army are here, and why you are interested in a routine commercial transaction?"

Marder only said, "You have no proof that you obtained this diamond from Moselle?"

"I don't need proof until you give me a reason. I am not even obligated to reveal my sources of merchandise. You need a subpoena if you want to force that kind of information. I did sell Bender a diamond. If he's not satisfied, that's completely outside of police jurisdiction. Let him give me back the diamond, and I'll get him his money."

Light laughed unpleasantly. I sneered in his face and added, "If Bender doesn't want to release the stone until I have the money, let him come uptown with me and we'll get it over with. But we'll have to work fast; the exchange closes at six." I looked at my watch – it was five already.

"*That* will be O.K. with me," Bender said, but he sounded strangely bitter.

I looked him in the eye now and I think it was a pretty good look. "Flaw or no flaw, that stone is a better buy than you'll ever know how to get again. I guaranteed your money back and that's the way it's going to be, but you got your money's worth." I raised my voice.

"*What did the diamond appraise for?*"

Marder answered. "It's worth about $21,000 plus tax at retail. The wholesale is $12,944."

I looked around the room at Marder's hatchet face, at Bender's narrow skull and close, mean eyes, at Light's mastiff head and face set for murder, at Bramson and Druckman's impassive cops' look, and I asked in wonder, "So what's the big war all about? I . . ."

But now something began to drill into me, a narrow beam, very hot, biting inside my skull. "What was that again, lieutenant? You said the wholesale was $12,944. How did you arrive at that exact figure?"

"From the invoice."

"*What invoice?*"

24

The room had a peculiar echo for such a small place, and I seemed to hear my voice repeating, *invoice*. Marder answered:

"Shenker and Krauskopf's. The bill paid to them by Henry Warrington & Co., March 28, 1959."

I did a little thinking. It wasn't easy. My head was holding nine cycles of thought. Ideas were circling like missiles. And a big one exploded. "You think that this is a diamond from the Warrington holdup?"

"It's been identified."

"That's out. There can be no identification of a diamond that will stand up against a man like Barney Moselle."

Marder wasn't impressed. "This one will. It has an unbroken history from South Africa to Israel to Shenker and Krauskopf to Warrington. It's been photographed microscopically, and the plates are certified by the government of Israel."

It sounded as if the stone had been meant for Queen Elizabeth's crown. I remarked, "Two men were killed in that holdup, weren't they?"

"And a policeman."

I tried to sound firm. "We better see Moselle. If he says no, your identification won't stand up – not against Moselle."

Druckman's voice came out, again from behind me:

"But against *you?*"

VII

It was past six when we reached Moselle's exchange:
Marder, Druckman, Bender, and myself. Marder had
phoned to make sure Moselle would be there. They kept
Light downtown. I didn't like that. He was the last man
to handle the stone, but it wouldn't make him feel kinder
toward me. Bender came along because I suggested it. If
I could, I was going to get him his money that night; I
didn't need any more of him.

Forty-seventh Street was quiet; only a few stragglers.
Lou Fogelman must have had a last rush; his salesman was
still pulling the window. Some of the big jewelry factories
were working overtime, high above our heads.

Henry let us in. Mrs. Moselle sat in a customer's high
chair before a counter: small, chic, intense. Barney held his
head steady a moment when he saw me; Mrs. Moselle
swept the incoming group with dark eyes. Moselle said
hello to Marder – the jewelry detail was nothing new to
him. Impassively he added, "Good evening, Saul, " and,
just as calmly, "Good evening, Mr. Bender."

"You know each other?" I asked.

"Mr. Bender has been pointed out to me. – Pleased to
meet you."

Bender's acknowledgment was surly. Funny how
different he looked to me now; three days ago a stinking
pal; now he loomed more like a cockroach on my pastrami.
One conviction was growing: Bender was a man many
people knew. The police certainly knew him.

Marder inspected the deserted exchange.

"Can we talk in your office, Mr. Moselle?"

"I've kept it open." He led the way through a room

26

consisting of a short passage between a blank wall and a huge pawnbroker's vault, complete with time lock. We entered an office, small but, considering the rent in that exchange, luxurious. It had heavy green carpeting, a large, dark wood desk, a filing cabinet, a small bar, several chairs, and a strongbox in the wall. The room was wired for Holmes protection, which gave him six systems against robbery: one on the exchange itself, one on the small safe behind the counters outside, a foot-lift alarm along the floor of each counter, a whole labyrinth of wires running through the concrete in which the big vault was set, the protection on the office as a whole, and an alarm under his desk. He would need three separate sets of signals from Holmes before he could go home. It wasn't too much; his inventory was in millions – he was ready to ship up to half a million dollars' worth of goods on consignment anywhere in the country upon receipt of a phone call from a responsible source. The bookkeepers, etc., occupied some rooms on the fourth floor.

He offered brandy. Everybody else declined. I accepted; I realized how good the idea was. We were seated loosely about the desk, Marder opposite Moselle. Marder exposed the diamond-paper and spread it open.

"Can you identify this?"

Moselle brought up his pocket glass and took tweezers from the desk drawer. The long chain attached to the glass lay across the desk when he leaned on his elbows. He looked at the gem lying in his paper, looked at me, and picked it up.

"I prefer daylight," he said, and he peered into the loupe.

As I said, Marder sat in front of him. I was at Moselle's right, Bender at Marder's, which put them opposite me, Druckman a little behind me as usual. I realized, as I tried to control my breathing, that Mrs. Moselle was also in the room, in the corner, behind Marder and opposite me. The fan from the air conditioner sang hoarsely; there was no other sound.

Moselle raised his head and met my eye. He went back to his studying, turning the diamond delicately from side to side. Then he stopped moving, and I could feel his eye plunging down the center. He made his decision, laid the stone carefully in the pan of the diamond scale at his left, and opening the little drawer beneath the balances, selected weights and placed them in the opposing pan. After adjusting the balance rod he released the lever which sets the indicator at the bottom tilted toward it. He moved the weight along the balance rod three points over – that's how close his first guess was; three one-hundredths of a carat. The pans came to rest with less motion than the veins in my temples, and the indicator quivered softly like a man long hung.

"Five-twenty-three," he remarked to nobody.

Marder nodded. He knew that. I said:

"You sold it to me for 5.21."

Moselle was quieter than the trembling brass fans:

"Not this one."

I leaned across the desk, and, so help me, Druckman got up and laid his hand, hard, on my shoulder.

"What do you mean – not this one?"

Druckman's fingers dug into my neck, as Moselle said:

"I have never seen this diamond before."

There is a saying, old as Cain, that the innocent have nothing to fear. There's not a word of truth in it. I was innocent, and I knew at that minute that I had as much to fear as one man can have. I wanted to speak up, clarify things, but I couldn't. I simply couldn't. I hadn't been three years a cop for nothing. Hell, I had made detective, lowest grade; one of the youngest on the Chicago force. My mind lined up the possibilities, the whole complex of crime and confusion; every chain of reasoning worked out, at once, in one second, to its paralyzing conclusion, and I understood what it must be like to be trapped in a time-locked vault over a long weekend. And through it one question, loud, harsh, kept pounding in my head: even if I *wasn't* held for murder, where was I going to get Bender's $16,000?

I eyed Bender. His entire being, the whole personality of the man had become a sinister sneer. I saw Druckman as I sank into my chair, baggy, bullying, happy and hateful. Marder sat three-quarter face, his forked chin pointing at that thin nose. Mrs. Moselle lay deep in a leather club chair; the glance she swung from her husband to me came out of the shadows like the dying spot on a fading television screen. I steadied my breath and turned to Moselle.

"Barney, do you realize what you are saying?"

He nodded gravely, his features inscrutable: wavy gray hair, broad pink forehead, mild eyes, a thick nose, full lips, some fat below the jaw. My life depended on what I could do with this casual acquaintance whom I called by his first name because everbody on Forty-seventh Street did that, to show you weren't nobody. But before I could say any more, Marder said:

"May I use your phone, Mr. Moselle?"

Moselle pushed it over to him. He dialed. I waited. "Bramson? . . . Release Light. . . . We have nothing to hold him on. . . . (He glanced at me.) Oh, maybe you better warn Light not to interfere in police business. He may be somewhat annoyed at our boy." He turned in his seat as he hung up. "We didn't have a choice, Mr. Bender. The goods were in his hands and three men's blood on it," All this very apologetically. He turned to me.

"You seem to be in disagreement with Mr. Moselle, Handy. You two old-time jewelry men don't see eye to eye. You didn't happen to have this five-carat stone in your possession, did you, when you accepted the other five-carat stone on Monday? So that the stones got mixed up? And, by the way, where *is* Mr. Moselle's 5.21 diamond? Has that one been turned over to another dealer? Have you made one sale or two?"

I was too clammy to sneer him down. I said:

"Barney, how can you be so sure that this isn't the diamond you gave me Monday?"

He answered as carefully as he had weighed the diamond, as carefully as a judge pronouncing sentence. "To begin with, Saul, the stone I gave you did not have a flaw. This one has a bubble at the culet. Secondly, my stone was of absolutely regular cut; I mentioned, I think, that it was cut like a diagram of a diamond. This stone is a fine-cut. This *is* just as good a diamond – maybe even a

29

little better than mine. Mr. Bender has an excellent buy here, if he can establish a clear title."

Bender leaped to his feet and came around the table to me.

"I've got a clear title to $15,937, you chiseling son-of-a-bitch, and I better have that money before I go out of here tonight."

"Before your Mr. Light sticks a knife into me."

He reached to grab the lapels of my coat. It was a bit repetitious. Druckman had had his hands on me lately and I was getting touchy. I had my right foot resting on my knee; when he came close, I pulled it tighter with my hands, and when he grabbed me I drove my shoe into his leg above the knee with all the power I could find. He spun crazily and fell on his face. Druckman sprang into action. I picked up a jade paperweight off Moselle's desk; the fathead actually reached for his gun.

Marder said, "Everybody sit down,"

The spots of light from Mrs. Moselle's corner hadn't flickered. Druckman sat down. I sat down, breathing heavily out of fear and rage. Bender got up limping; his face spelled murder.

The fat was really in the fire. I doubted if even his money back would keep me alive.

VIII

I must have needed badly to kick somebody; my head was clear now. I was ready to begin for the defense. I turned to Marder;

"I would like to go into this with Mr. Moselle a little deeper."

"Meaning?"

"Ask some questions."

Druckman let out a horselaugh. "We need him."

"It will only take a few minutes. I want to go over everything which took place between us two last Monday."

Druckman said, "I would like to go over Mr. Handy a little, downtown."

By now I had the coolness of the doomed.

"The lieutenant isn't going to book me."

"No?" Marder inquired.

"On what?"

"Possession."

"You'll have to include Bender and Light, and, I think, Moselle. If you can't hold Light, you can't hold me. That's exactly why I want to ask some questions."

"I don't get you."

"Since you can't hold Light, you can't hold Bender. And with those two hoodlums loose, you can't protect me. That's if you wanted to."

"We can protect you."

I jerked my thumb at Druckman. "With *this?*"

I heard Druckman's chair moving, and I got up turning. "Don't try anything, fat boy, unless you're going all the way."

"Sit down." Marder said.

31

After we sat down I said to Marder, "And you better run a check on me. You'll find I am an ex-policeman with an excellent record, City of Chicago. You'll find that I come from Springfield, Illinois, that my father was in the jewelry business in Springfield for forty years: a substantial merchant. You'll find a perfect army record. MP. Went in private, came out sergeant. And you'll find I have an Illinois license as a private detective.

"Mr. Bender also comes from Illinois. His father was an honest plumber. I don't know if Mr. Bender is an honest anything, but I think you do.

"You'll realize, after the checkout, that I only have two things to worry about: my reputation in the jewelry business and certain well-connected gangsters. It will also sink in that I can't be intimidated by police routine, either your kind or his," and I jerked my thumb at Druckman again.

Marder had been studying me throughout that speech. He looked very unfriendly. He began:

"In this town, we don't like ex-policemen who get mixed up with murder. Especially, ex-cops with meaningless, out-of-state licenses."

"How about big-shot racketeers from the same state who come in here and clean up millions? And how about policemen on active duty who get mixed up with them?"

Marder was reaching the limit of his control. "Ask your questions."

I took in a lungful of what air there was. "Barney, I need your help. I need your active co-operation – your mind. I want you to help me trace the history of that damned diamond you gave me, second by second, and inch by inch."

"Anything I can, Saul."

"First, from whom did you get the diamond you sold me?"

"I imported it directly from Holland."

"When?"

"During the summer. I've had it maybe three months."

"Was it part of a larger shipment?"

"Yes."

"You keep a description of each diamond you handle?"

"Pretty close. Always of imports."

"What information do you record?"

"Weight, color, cut, quality."

"Quality only means perfect or imperfect?"

"We go into more detail: perfect, V.V.S., V.S., P.K." (V.V.S. means very, very slightly imperfect; P.K. means decidedly defective, showing carbon spots or other prominent flaws.)

"So if you consult your records you will presumably find the stone you sold me entered as color, very fine; cut, regular; quality, perfect?"

"That's right."

I thought a minute. The spot of light from Mrs. Moselle's chair was fixed on me.

"Do you take a Moe gauge reading of each stone?"

"What for? I have the weight?"

"That's right. But do you happen to have a Moe gauge reading of the stone we are talking about?"

"No. Why are you interested in that?"

"A Moe gauge reading would show that the stone you gave me was a fine-cut."

"You're wasting your time, Saul."

Marder cut in. "And ours. Step on it."

All right, Barney, let's try something else. How many times was the stone I paid for out on memo? I realize you don't keep a record; I only want your estimate."

"You can have an exact answer. It never left the store until you took it."

Druckman grunted. My legs turned cold. Even Marder was startled. Bender's lips moved in a silent curse. Marder said slowly:

"You should have let the New York police department handle this investigation."

I fought off the numbness. "How can you be sure?"

"I am sure."

"Couldn't Henry have given it out? You don't check every memo."

"I look them over."

"Couldn't you forget it afterwards?"

"On that size stone? Maybe a year later."

33

"Suppose when you were away from business – vacation or something?"

"I haven't missed a day since that diamond was received."

Marder said, "You must have built up some wonderful cases while you were in Chicago."

Druckman added, "This guy checked pushcart licenses."

Bender got up. "I'm going. I've had enough. I have to meet my wife."

"See Mr. Bender to the door, Druckman. Sorry we've inconvenienced you."

Bender answered nobody and looked at nobody. I watched his back going through the door and Druckman with him. "Mr. Big goes to dinner," I said pleasantly to Marder. "What is he – bossman in the syndicate?"

"He was your friend, wasn't he?"

"I knew him in Springfield."

"You'll know him in hell the way you're going."

I turned back to Moselle. He was all I had left. "Now, Barney, you do have other diamonds very similar in size and quality to the one you sold me."

"Yes, Saul," Moselle said almost sadly, "I do. But you know well enough that I can tell my diamonds apart."

He certainly could. A man like Moselle knows his stones so well he can recognize one after not seeing it for five years – so they tell me. I went on:

"I want you to think carefully, Barney. Can you say how many stones you have between, say five carats fifteen points and five carats thirty, the quality comparable to the Dutch diamond?"

"You mean on hand tonight?"

"I mean particularly on hand last Monday noon."

He looked rather surprised. "Only one, now that I think of it."

"Why didn't you show it to me?"

"It wasn't perfect."

"How do you know this one isn't it? You could have made a mistake."

Moselle sighed. "I've already said I've never seen this stone. And I don't make such mistakes. The other one is

34

a diamond of not more than 5.20. Five-eighteen, I think. The flaw is not so far down and is more off center. Besides, it's a coarse-cut, not a fine-cut."

"How long have you had it?"

"Oh, several years."

"It's been out on consignment?"

"Often, I imagine. It's certainly been out."

"Is it here now?"

"Yes."

"Could I see it?"

He rapped his fingers up and down on the desk. Marder said, "You don't have to if you don't want to, Mr. Moselle."

"Barney," I said, "I've got a lot at stake."

He looked at me with an expression I couldn't read. "Something told me," he remarked, "to keep the vault open tonight." And he got up and left the room.

Tense as I was, I found myself covertly studying Mrs. Moselle. Bender had left, no doubt to brief his killers; Druckman was behind me again; Moselle had gone through the door; but her eyes had never gone away from me. I must have had something for her; horror, no doubt; I *was* the youngest and best-looking man in the room, but that wasn't saying much.

Moselle came back and laid a paper on the desk.

"Just a minute," Marder cut in sharply. He reached over, carefully wrapped up the stolen diamond, and put it in his pocket. "Now go ahead."

Moselle exposed the diamond and pushed it toward me. Lying under that intense bluish light, it was a beauty; so much like the other one that I didn't blame Marder for taking no chances with his evidence. I took the tweezers, picked it up, and asked Moselle for a glass. Marder handed me his.

I wished I didn't look so much like a damned amateur, trying to handle the tweezers in front of two such men. What a color that stone had! Just as good, to me, as the one I gave Bender. But as I looked, and I was really looking, I began to feel a strange excitement.

"Barney—" I guess my voice was vibrant – "Barney, I don't see the flaw."

"Just below the girdle, Saul, halfway off center."

"To me, it's perfect."

He gave me a sympathetic smile and took the stone. He looked and looked. I looked at him and then at Marder. Marder was quietly watching the show, the lamp flooding Moselle's bent gray head and the bit of fire, a centimeter from his eye.

I gave him plenty of time and then I said, "Would you call that stone a coarse-cut?"

"No," he answered slowly, "I wouldn't."

"Doen't that stone exactly match the description you gave me of the Dutch diamond?"

Moselle sat back in his chair, laying the diamond on the desk. "Yes, Saul, it does."

We all looked gravely at the star of the show: half an inch of beauty flickering in its paper on the black surface of the desk like a tiny ballerina under a spotlight. Marder took out the other diamond and carefully laid it near its sister. The two prima donnas were six inches away, two stars of the same magnitude, alone in a wide, dark sky.

Then I said, "Barney, I'm positive you didn't loupe the diamond when you showed it to me Monday."

He nodded, "It didn't seem necessary – but you did."

"That's right; I did. But what does that mean? It's all I could do to find the flaw after Marder pointed it out to me. You find what you look for. Since you said it was perfect, that settled it for me. I looked for perfection. As for the cut, I never examined the cut at all, and I wouldn't argue with a man like you, ordinarily, even if I did think it was a fine. You said regular; I saw regular. I even sold it for a regular, but I never studied it from that point of view."

"One thing is left," Moselle observed. He picked up his diamond and put it on the scale. The weights from the Israeli diamond were still in the pan and the balance weight stood at twenty-three points. "This one is marked five-eighteen," he pointed out.

When Moselle released the balances, they held steady, steadier than my breath, the diamond above the weights and the indicator tilted to correspond. Moselle delicately moved the balance two points, and the pans swung dead level.

"Five-twenty-one?" I asked superfluously.

He nodded. He was studying the writing on the outside of the diamond-paper where dealers record the details about the contents.

"It must have got into the wrong paper," I said carefully, as if my words would shatter the stone.

"Yes," said Moselle, "it must have. I'm sorry, Saul."

At last Marder spoke. "It's interesting. But how does that explain Handy's possession of this stolen merchandise?

"It doesn't," I said amiably. "It doesn't *explain* it. But it certainly affects it. If fifty people have handled the paper which held the stone I bought, and if the stone I took out hasn't been checked against these specifications during repeated handling, anybody at all might have substituted that stolen diamond for the one Moselle doesn't have. The point is Moselle is short one stone, and since there has been confusion in the handling, he doesn't know how long he has missed it. He *may* have given it to me Monday, but he can't be sure. All he knows is that he gave me whatever stone was in that paper," and I pointed to the paper which held the hot goods.

"The switch," I added, "may have been done accidentally or on purpose, by anybody who had the missing stone on memo; or it may have been done by Barney himself, or by any of his employees, or by a sleight-of-hand artist over the counter, or by Bender or by Light."

"Or by you," Marder contributed. "Do you expect Mr. Moselle to refund all that money on the strength of nothing more than this?

He may not have realized he was conceding he couldn't hold me. But to answer his question I looked at Moselle's kindly, tired, distinguished face. "You don't know Barney Moselle, lieutenant. He might do just that."

Marder was watching Moselle curiously (so was Mrs. Moselle). He said to me, "In the meantime, what are your plans for Ed Bender?"

Then I leaned toward Marder and leered into his eyes. "No, lieutenant – not what are my plans. What are your plans? How do you plan to protect me? I do appreciate that you must handle Mr. Bender with kid gloves – with a chamois, in fact. I now appreciate what a big man Mr. Bender is in the eyes of the department. God only knows, and maybe the commissioner, all that Mr. Bender does for the department. But I expect you to keep me alive, lieutenant, even against Mr. Bender. Mr. and Mrs. Moselle are witnesses to this business. They know, and I will let others know, that if I'm not safe in this town, it's because you didn't dare take the necessary steps."

Marder's thin face was as cold as the edge of a knife. "Are you trying to imply that the police connive at murder?"

"I'll soon know," I said agreeably. "So will everybody in this room. And I can talk to a few more in the time I have left."

I got up. "And now, if you don't mind, I, who am about to die, am going home. I leave you and your charming associate. I'm a bit tired of all this; cops, robbers, stolen goods, threats, violence. I wasn't raised in it."

Druckman was up and ready to block me but Marder waved him away. I never did find out what Druckman contributed to that team. I added something: "You might begin by phoning the distinguished citizen who has just left us. Suggest to him that it might be better to let me live until we see how things work out. My corpse will never pay off."

"Don't leave town," Marder said affably.

"Wouldn't think of it. Good-by, Barney. Thanks for everything."

"I'll probably phone you tomorrow," Marder said as I went through the door ahead of Druckman.

Tomorrow? When was that? Was I going back to Corbin's tomorrow? Do a day's work? Give out goods on memo?

Mrs. Moselle sat in her corner, her eyes concentrated and enormous. I went out of the room, the exchange, and that world, into a dark, dead Forty-seventh Street.

IX

An hour later I went into the White Lily. Nine hundred restaurants within a block of where I stood and I picked that dump. I was't in a mood to celebrate. None of the little French restaurants on Forty-ninth Street meant a thing to me. I didn't feel like sampling Cantonese, Pakistani, or Armenian cooking either. I didn't even want borscht and herring.

I had walked steadily for the hour. I had gone east almost to the river and west almost to *that* river. I had dreamed my way past the world of Manhattan's cooking and I ended up with a London broil on rye and a stein of ale.

Rose was on. I hadn't expected her; she didn't work nights, but the manager had asked her to help him. Rose is blond (at least to the eye), round, solid, and mature. I was glad to see her. An eon had passed since I had left her tip at three o'clock that same day.

"What's new?" she said.

"Nothing."

She decided to grace my table, so she slipped onto the bench opposite.

"I have a picture of him if you want to try."

I laughed. I laughed loud. "You have a mug shot! Bring it in, so I can go up and see him sometime."

She shoved her hand into her black uniform and came out with a photo. He wasn't a bad-looking guy. Rather tall as far as I could judge, thiry-five or less, and a bit fleshy. It didn't seem to be a picture of a happy man.

"What does he do?"

"He's an artist."

39

"Commercial? Comics, illustrations, advertising – that stuff?"

"He does abstractions. Is that commercial?"

"And how. Could I keep this a few days?" With nothing on my mind but murder, it was what I needed. As I mentioned, I'm also a schmuck.

"Yes," she said tentatively. "But take care of it."

"As if it were a five-carat pear-shape, with only one small flaw. What's his name?"

"Robert Karl."

It sounded better and better. "I'll call him Bud. You never asked him where he lived?"

"He doesn't live there."

I took another stein of ale. I was tired and the ale turned my legs to zinc. I settled with Rose and went out into the beauty of Sixth Avenue. I was pretty sure I could find her jerk if he was a New York abstract expressionist. It would be like finding the guy who had to live in Greenwich Village: he couldn't afford the rents anywhere else – down there he could live like a queen. Abstract expressionists are in a few places; I knew this because I had a friend who painted. I had an idea my friend could recognize Rose's Bud or could tell me who would.

It was cooler. Sixth Avenue stank like the city jail: gas fumes, beer, garbage, slums, and the human species. The overflow from the jewelry block ran up and down the avenue for a short way. It was distasteful to me; the whole gold-plated, iridium-platinum, cultured pearl, blue-white racket was like something sticking to my breath.

I didn't see anybody who looked as though he wanted to kill me. I didn't know what to do with myself. I had had all the entertainment I could use for one day. Corbin's, the White Lily, the police department, Moselle's, Rose – it was enough. But I didn't want to go back to my hotel.

For the first time I wished I had a wife.

I decided to get my car out of the lot and take a drive. Maybe I would go to Coney Island; it shouldn't be crowded so late in September. The reek of fish and salt water might clear my lungs. Phoniness in Coney Island is in the open; they don't Florentine it.

The lot, only a block from Moselle's, was badly lighted. I looked for Moselle's Cadillac as I walked through. I didn't see it; undoubtedly the Moselles had more than one car anyhow.

I edged my car through the one-way side street and onto Seventh Avenue. I didn't much care where I went or how I got there, but I thought I would go a ways down Fifth Avenue. The lights stopped me before I could turn east. I looked. I looked in front of me, dull and dreary, and noticed the traffic cop gesticulating foolishly at somebody. He started to run; I couldn't care less; but then a lot of people were hollering and the blue uniform came up to my window.

"Anything wrong, officer?"

"Open your door," and he backed away.

I opened it, looked at him, and looked where he pointed. My rear door was sticking out like a banner.

"Oh, dear," I said brightly. "How could that happen?"

The policeman was a tall young man, very good-looking. He stared at me as if I were swallowing a sword. I got out, feeling excessively foolish, and then I saw it, the body, half in the car, and half, the upper half, trailing into the street. God knows how far I had dragged it.

Nobody said anything that I heard – not one of a hundred people who could see me. I went closer to the thing on the pavement, and as I did the rest of it slid out. It lay face up. mouth open, eyes open, one arm stuck out and pointing at me, and it didn't look alive. After a second or two, I recognized it

Someone pulled my arm. "Don't touch anything," the policeman said. "Stop your motor."

I reached into the car and shut the motor off. The cop held out his hand; I gave him the keys. There were two more cops now.

"Who's your friend?" one of them asked.

I pondered the question. "He was no friend of mine."

"Know him?"

"Yes. His name is Light. I don't know what he was doing in my car."

The two new cops were looking inside. There was

considerable blood on the seat, the floor, the door, and on the corpse.

"You don't know what he was doing there?"

"No," I said slowly.

"I do," the tall young one remarked.

I fell for it. "What?"

"Dying."

X

"Didn't you say you were going some place?" Marder asked when I entered the interrogation room.

I didn't answer. The room was exactly like the first one. It held three homicide dicks, Marder, and Druckman. Less than five hours had passed since my last visit. I was very much under arrest.

"How the hell, " Druckman asked, "do you expect to get out of this one?"

"I *may* have an alibi," I answered gravely.

I sat down where I was told, opposite a gray, harsh homicide man, even bigger than Al Light. His name was Cassidy – Sergeant Cassidy.

Druckman went on. "Maybe he was in the car all the time."

"He certainly didn't go far," Marder agreed.

The homicide man said, "I would like to go over your movements from the time you left Lieutenant Marder until you were stopped opposite the Astor with that corpse trailing out of your car."

"It wasn't exactly opposite the Astor. I was on the east side of Seventh Avenue. I left Moselle's about 7:15. I was stopped at 9:09. You want an account of my time for one hour and fifty-four minutes."

"That's about it," Cassidy said.

"If it's not too much trouble," said Druckman. "He's a very busy guy."

"Actually we don't need all that time," Marder said."-Light didn't leave here until 7:15. Giving him time to get to your car, the earliest you could have made contact was about 7:35."

I was calculating quietly. I had done nothing else since I had grasped my situation more than an hour ago. We had hung around Forty-fifth Street and Seventh Avenue while the homicde boys came up, while routine inquiries were made, and until the arresting officer had managed to find a newspaper photographer to take his picture. Television had not been available at the moment, but I was going to be a famous man on Forty-seventh Street tomorrow.

"Let's hear about 7:35," Cassidy suggested. "And after."

I answered slowly. "At 7:35 I was walking. I walked around aimlessly trying to get fresh air into my blood. I first went east, all the way to the river. When I saw the water, I thought what a good place that would be to dispose of my body if friends were following me, so I turned and walked back."

"Were you gong to turn east on Forty-fourth Street?" Cassidy asked. "Later – when you were driving?"

"Yes," I answered, surprised. "I was."

"The river would be a good place for Light's body, wouldn't it?"

"Not at all." I said coldly. "The best place would be Bender's front yard in Crestmere."

"Can't think of everything," Cassidy observed. "After all, you hadn't much time. The fact that you didn't close your door properly shows you were not thinking clearly."

"I guess," said Druckman, "he made no mistake giving up police work."

Cassidy nodded. "Doesn't improvise well."

"I wouldn't have a chance," I said, "in the kind of company I've seen around here."

"We're not so good as Chicago," Cassidy said. "But we'll sew up this one."

"You have done the obvious things," I pointed out. "You found a man with a hot diamond and you held him. You asked him who he got it from and you held *that* one. Your case blew up so you released both men. When the second man dragged the corpse of the first one in front of your face, you started all over again. Nothing wrong with your moves, but I doubt if they will write it up in any police manuals."

"The crime itself won't get written up for brilliance either," Cassidy said. "Christ, if you were going to claim self-defense, what did you move him around for?"

Marder cut in. "Who saw you while you were surveying the town? Speak to anybody?"

"No," I answered. "I wasn't looking for conversation."

"How long did you walk?"

"About an hour. I went into the White Lily restaurant on Sixth Avenue near 8:30."

"Nobody will remember that either?"

"Oh, yes, they will. The waitress will remember me perfectly."

"When did you leave the White Lily?"

"I don't know. I went straight to the parking lot, got into my car, and pulled out. Must have left the restaurant around 8:55."

"Quick work," said Cassidy. "You were stopped at 9:09. Did anybody see you enter the parking lot?"

"The attendant – if he remembers."

"Anybody else?"

"Not that I know of."

"Who's this? handing me the picture of Rose's painter. (They had searched me, of course.)

"Robert Karl."

"Where does he live?"

"I don't know. It's not my photo."

"Whose is it?"

"The waitress's at the White Lily."

"What's he to you?"

"Nothing."

"Why are you carrying it?"

"I'm to show it to another painter."

And then, very tough, *"What did you do with the weapon?"*

It went on for two hours. No lamp though, no rough stuff, just steady questions. Then they left me alone for a while.

I wasn't worried too much about the murder rap. The blood on my car was fresh – no drying at all. They would wait for the lab report. I had had only fourteen minutes to walk two blocks, find Light, kill him, get my car out of the lot, and get to Forty-sixth Street in traffic. There wasn't a mark on me when I was arrested – not a bit of blood or a trace of struggle. If Light had died in the car just before they spotted me, then, as I figured it, they wouldn't hold me. If he had been put into the car already dead, they might suspect me either of being an accessory or of killing him in a fight. Even then I doubted if they would make a charge unless they found some corroboration.

The questions I had to answer were: who did kill Light? Had they meant to kill me? Why my car? Was Light waiting to get me when he got it? What did Bender have to do with it? Why such a risky place as a parking lot? What did Bender intend to do about me and his $16,000 – not counting a kick in the knee and whatever Light was worth to him if he did think I had killed him?

By one o'clock they had their reports, and had undoubtedly made a first check at the White Lily. They began to look like wolves on the wrong side of the sheepfold. I felt I could ask some questions:

"Do you have the time of death?"

"He was still bleeding when you stopped the car."

"What I like about this guy," Druckman said, "is that he always stops for a red light."

I asked, "Was there any blood in the parking lot?"

"Not that we've found so far. You began to leave a trail on Seventh Avenue near Forty-sixth. Your door must have opened when you turned into Seventh Avenue."

"You figure he was killed in my car?"

"What do you think?"

"I would say so. What was the murder weapon?"

"A blunt instrument. A heavy one, like an iron pipe or a tire iron. Not a wooden club."

"Find it?"

It was a foolish question. Cassidy ignored it.

"Turning me loose?"

He adjusted his heavy body to his clothes and his chair. His look was sour. "May we wait a little? At the rate you come up, you'll be back before breakfast anyway."

"How long?"

"Want to call a lawyer?"

I thought about it. To begin with, I don't know any lawyers.

"Not until morning," I decided. "I would like to make a call at nine o'clock if you haven't released me by then."

"Get room service," Cassidy said to his helper. They gave me a uniformed man who took me to a cell. I doubted that they made entries – just provided the room. Police stations are not so strict about registering guests.

Everybody knows what a cell is like. Mine was no different. I went through the night. By eight o'clock in the morning I was eating breakfast on the jewelry block in Nassau Street. Like Maiden Lane and Forty-seventh Street, it was home – all the home I had.

XI

I went to work as usual. It was the only thing to do. The Corbins had evidently seen the papers; they looked up at me politely.

"Shall I start?"

Jake lifted his eyebrows and his hands.

"Why not?"

"There might be a corpse in the men's room."

"Rough night, huh?"

"Rough."

"What next?"

"I don't know. I'll go around to Moselle's after I put the stuff out."

"Take the ring mandril if you need a blunt instrument." They knew nothing about the stolen diamond, nor did the papers apparently.

I arranged the goods for half an hour and went into the street, partly to avoid conversation with the first batch of Indians coming through the door. There was a chill in the air, like homicide. I caught a glimpse of the White Lily as I went into the exchange.

Henry was already writing a memo. "Good morning, Saul," he said politely as if he couldn't read newsprint, but of course his customer, Abe Yamaka, could be depended upon to come out with, "A little trouble, Saul?"

"Not really,"I answered shortly. "Barney in?"

Henry picked up the phone. "Mr. Handy to see Mr. Moselle." He hung up. A few seconds later, after the call went up to the fourth floor and down to Moselle, Henry's phone rang.

"Take Mr. Handy into Mr. Moselle's office," Henry

called to one of his assistants (he had at least five). We went past the vaults. The huge outer doors were open; the inner ones locked. Moselle got up to say hello, which is probably his custom for everybody. I sat down facing him in the chair Marder had used the night before.

We exchanged looks. Barney Moselle was about fifty or maybe a little more: gray-eyed, no glasses, pink skin as I have said, a certain fineness and kindness about him. It was a face which would show suffering if the man ever were to suffer.

I am rather short, very undistinguished-looking, brown hair, blue eyes, roundish, and not good to hang clothes on. Each of us thought the other honest, but neither of us knew where that broke off.

Moselle said, "I did not know." he went on, "at the beginning of the week that we would become so well acquainted."

"You can say hello to a guy for a long time," I said, "and not much more."

"It's like merchandise. It lies around and you never really look at it. What happened after we left here?"

"The papers have the gist of it – leaving out my feelings."

"Yes," he said, "your feelings. I'm trying to estimate your feelings."

"We all have them. Mine seem important to me."

We said nothing for half a minute. Then he asked, "What's next?"

"That's what I have to figure."

"Do the police think you killed Light?"

"They probably think he was trying to pressure me and that I took him by surprise."

"But they have released you."

"They don't have enough. No weapon, no clear motive, no time. They may pick me up again after they work on it. What has saved me so far is the blood. If I had had a drop of it on me, I'd be meat for the district attorney."

"A terrible situation."

"I'll survive. My biggest worry is Bender and his money."

His face barely changed. We had got down to business.

49

I couldn't help thinking how different the business was for the two of us. He had a matter of legal rights, commercial ethics, and, just possibly, personal ethics. The sum of money in itself was a routine business risk which he assumed every hour. For me, the money was beyond all possible reach. Nothing that could happen to me in all my life would enable me to come by it.

"Bender," he said, "is certainly entitled to his money. You *may* be entitled to yours. It's not a nice thing."

I said nothing. What for? Moselle went on: My position is awkward. I'm in a business of giving out large amounts on consignment. The sacredness of memos is everything to me. You remember the Flack case?"

I remembered. Flack had sold $100,000 worth of goods, obtained on memo, and he hadn't paid for the stones. He wasn't entirely without resources, and he could have settled up a lot of it in time. Maybe one third of the merchandise came from Moselle. The other creditors were willing to wait and settle for possibly 60 per cent, but Barney had figured that it was more important for him to be known as a man whose memos were untouchable. He had prosecuted and put Flack in jail at a net cost of some $20,000.

"This," Moselle observed, "is a case of a lost stone. Even if the stone wasn't the one I said it was, I'm entitled to get it back, if I'm to return the money. If I give back the money every time somebody loses a stone, I won't be able to close up fast enough.'

"And," I said, "this is one very lost stone. Warrington may get it someday, but nobody else. A cop died over that diamond. The trail of blood runs like a river. And it all runs on me. I'm so smeared by it now that if Bender decides to bump me off, I'll be afraid to defend myself.'

"You think that is likely?"

I should have said yes; if I had, I think he would have given me a check then and there. But I couldn't – not quite – so I said:

"I don't think so. Too obvious and too useless. Some form of pressure is certain. The very least is a judgment which would haunt me from job to job for the rest of my life."

Moselle took his elbows off the desk. "Shall we have some coffee?"

"I don't really feel like it,"

He let go the phone, "Are you working now?"

"I started as usual,"

"The Corbins act normal?"

"Terribly. Of course, all they know about is the murder. Merchandise might be a different story."

"It might be wise to stay with them until things clear up."

He was telling me. I didn't answer and he said, "I want a little time to study all the angles to this case. You really were a policeman once?"

"Oh, yes. Now I wish I had stayed at it."

His phone rang. He talked business for a minute, and said, "I'll come out," Then he said to me, "Saul, I want to see you some place where we can talk. Could you come to my apartment?"

"Why not? When?"

"How about tonight?"

"I'll be there."

"Come for dinner."

"I'd rather not. Wrong mood. Would eight o'clock suit you?"

"If you're sure you won't eat with us." He paused. "I – it's important that our talk be strictly confidential for reasons that you will understand quickly enough, so please don't say anything about the appointment."

We shook hands and went out of the office together, I a little more bewildered than when I went in. The exchange was already humming with autumn shoppers. I avoided everybody I knew until I reached the street, where the inevitable character, in this case an old freak known as Stony Schulz (he was a lapidary) yelled out, "How's everything, Saul?" I kept on moving. I don't know why, of all the stonecutters in New York, he should be called Stony.

It was too early for beer or for eating, but I went into the White Lily anyhow. I deserved a little time off, even if I hadn't killed anybody. Rose was in her unappetizing black uniform. In deference to the early hour, I took Virginia ham on a roll, after which she said:

"Do anything about him yet?"

I put my hand in my coat pocket; the photo was there. I had completely forgotten the jerk. The police had probably made a copy, found him, and gone over him for matching blood.

"Rose," I said, "did you see the papers?"

She turned pale. "Have they found him?"

"Not him, Rose. Me."

She relaxed. "What about you?"

"I've been busy."

"I'm sorry."

"You're forgiven. I may soon have lots of time to work on your business."

"Are you having trouble?"

"Nothing that will bother me in six hundred years. By the way, I don't think you'll be seeing the man from the numbers racket."

"Why?"

"A hunch. If you notice a replacement, let me know,"

As soon as I went back to work I saw it was going to be one of those days. Ada Mann was waiting, and she spent thirty-five minutes by the clock before she could bring herself to sign up for a tree-of-life and a sample calendar. And the chop, chop chop! She would eventually get an order for the calendar and return the two pieces, neither of them any newer for her care, total sale $4.40, gross profit to us 85 cents.

Then the rush began, and I didn't get off my feet until 2:30. I ate in a Chinese place, mostly to avoid Rose.

The complaints are the worst of our business. Each of our customers is an expert on something, and you can tell what he does by what he cries about. Our finishing hasn't been too good lately, and the gossiping over the engine-turning, the polishing, the Florentining, the satin finishing, the sand-blasting, is something to listen to – polished finish is a mirror-like surface, engine-turning is highly polished grooving, satin finish is an emery-rubbed surface, Florentine is fine scratching, brushed gold is a smoother Florentine, sand-blasted an extremely dull effect, almost no reflection, chiefly used on men's rings. Since all dull finishes become polished by wear and all polished finishes become dull from scratches, you have an interminable source of grief. I was over my ears in it; I washed it off with little cups of oolong and thought about Barney Moselle wanting to see me at his home. There was no answer in the tea leaves, so I returned to Corbin's, dodging a lot of well-wishers in the trade, and finished the day.

I had barely said good night and got into the street when someone tapped my shoulder. I turned stiff, but it wasn't from Bender; it was only the law.

"Good evening, sergeant," I said cheerfully. "Taking a recount?"

Cassidy didn't bother to say good evening. "Let's sit down," he said, pointing to a prowl car, parked by a fire hydrant near Gondarian's store. The Armenian's head was still sticking into his window as he picked up the rings, mounted on large price cards which challenged comparisons, demanded appraisals, and certified bargains. I went into the car with Cassidy while his partner stood on the sidewalk, leaning against the open window and enjoying the foul air.

We were crowded; Cassidy is a tremendous man. The car stank slightly, as a police car will; God knows what they may have to haul off in those buggies – police work is not fumigated. I looked into Cassidy's blue eyes and reflected how awful it would be to look like that. He said:

"You do pretty well with the girls, Handy"

Now I studied him. "Meaning?"

"Just that. I presume there are women in your life."

"Not enough of them." I meant it. As a matter of fact, New York is not the best town in the world for a single guy with few friends. I could have more women in a week in Springfield than I could find in a month in New York. And New York is a high-priced place. Still I do get around some. I waited for Cassidy's next witticism.

"I want a list of your girl friends," he said, just like that.

I put my hand in my pocket. "I don't seem to have my address book. You must have neglected to return it to me when I left your establishment. Might I ask what you want with the history of my sex life?" Believe me, I was trying to think.

"I don't need the ancient history." He paused, breathed, blew his nose, and went on. "I want a list of the ones who have been in your car. It's a new car; how many can there be?"

I sat quiet in the darkening street and digested the information. Cassidy had given me a lot of information – more than he knew of, because I knew what he didn't. Finally he said:

"Do you need a pencil and paper?"

"You, I said, "have found something in the car pertaining to a woman. Is it something that was sticking to the corpse?"

"It was something that is going to stick you back in jail if you don't own up."

There were two problems: (1) How could I get him to tell me exactly what he had found? (2) If I told him the truth, how would I make him believe it? For the truth was, there never had been, to my knowledge, a woman in that car. I had had the Olds only three months. I had not been out of the city since the week of July Fourth, when Forty-seventh street shuts down, and that week I hadn't ridden any dames around. I had no steady girl friend; the few women I had been with lived near my hotel and had rooms of their own. Ten thousand women in a radius of one mile – my car was strictly for business and fresh air. I like a car *after* a woman. But what cop would believe that the Olds was a virgin, especially if they had found a lipstick or something. I said:

"You didn't turn up anything very bulky or you'd have said something last night."

"Not very bulky, Men have been hung on less."

"So what's the mystery? What did you find?"

Cassidy got red. His skin was no cold cream ad, red or white, but maybe the red was worse. "Don't I talk plain, feller? What women have been in that car since you bought it? Or do we go downtown? Christ! You were found with the body; I don't have to play up to you."

Not one thing had broken my way that week; as the boys in the exchanges say, everything I had touched had turned to something soft. I went stubborn.

"Do what you damn please. Either you lay your cards on the table or I don't say one more word."

The other detective's face was coming through the window. He was a lean, mean character, a regular television cop. Cassidy raised his eyes slightly. "Get inside, Tommy," he snarled. He was breathing hard.

Cassidy reached for the ignition. Tommy got in back. Cassidy put his hand back on his knee; I saw his mind change. He said:

"There are two kinds of blood. One was a woman's."

Now I was breathing. "How the hell can you tell it was a woman's? You must have found fingerprints."

From behind, Tommy said, "We're recruiting men from all over the damned country and we pass up a prospect like this. Let's sign him up before Chicago sends for him."

"Yeah," said Cassidy, "a natural detective. We have two kinds of blood, fingerprints, perfume, powder, and a shred of tie silk that didn't come off no tie. Now, Mr. Handy, who was she?"

It was the year of the tie-silk dresses. I said:

"I have never had a woman in that car."

Cassidy turned on the ignition and started the motor. Tommy said, "Some co-operation."

I said, "That's the exact truth: not one woman,"

From the back, "It's going to be fun breaking the bridge of this bastard's nose."

I said, "I knew you wouldn't believe me."

"If that was the truth," Cassidy said bitterly, "you wouldn't have played it so cute. That car's tied into a cop-killing."

"That's why I played it the way I did. I would never have found out what you had if I had told you the truth first. And I have to have what you have."

He shut off the motor. "Why do you have to have what we have?"

"Don't you think I'm an interested party?"

"Are you planning to investigate this case on your own?"

"I think I have a right to look around."

He took the trouble to twist his thick neck and exchange glances with his partner. "Handy," he said, "don't make a mistake about this. You'll keep your hands entirely out of police business. All you will do is answer questions. For as long as you can. For as long as till we break you in half or some of Light's pals get you. I think you killed Light. I might make a deal with you about that if you'll come clean with all you know about the Warrington holdup. I know you're lying right now. If you make one move to interfere with us, I'll slap you in jail on a list of charges as long as your arm."

He could do it. Even if I was granted bail, it would have been hard as hell to raise it. And jewelry men are supposed to stay out of jail. We went over the ground a few more times, me wondering what the chances were that partner would suddenly club me over the head for resisting arrest, now that the street was very dark and empty. Then Cassidy said, "Get out of this car.'

He pulled away quickly, very dissatisfied. I felt like a Staten Island ferryboat in a tropical hurricane. I was shaking, but that was for extra; I would have been stunned by the news in any case.

Light and some woman had been in my car. Light had bled and died there; the woman had bled and gone, dead or alive. Why? Who? Had she been in on Light's killing? Had they both been murdered and had she been hauled away? Did I know her? Had Light been waiting to murder me? Had she killed Light by mistake? And Bender? I reflected that I should have asked Cassidy what kind of perfume.

I hoped she hadn't been killed. I didn't want the only girl to have sat in my new car to be a dead one. The last lights went out along the street. It was seven o'clock, too early for Moselle. I walked slowly up Sixth Avenue, half conscious, went into a bar on Forty-ninth, had two shots of whisky, and took a cab. I reached Moselle's address on Central Park West about fifteen minutes ahead of time wondering at my own strength.

XII

The building was big, one of those good older structures still standing along the lower end of Central Park West. A sharp wind blew in from the park; I could have used a topcoat. Central Park lay dark and glamorous; a lovely estate, suitable for a king's preserve, now given over to brigands and wild beasts.

The avenue was filled with cars, which stopped and went on, gathered riders and let them go; everything well polished and smartly dressed. The people were sleek and forceful, like their cars; it wasn't Park Avenue but it had something Park Avenue doesn't have – more beauty in the setting and perhaps more drive in the actors. These scarred, hard people had come up, not been up – they were absolutely New York.

I went past a busy doorman into an old-fashioned lobby with marble pillars, a switchboard, three elevators, and period furniture. The chandeliers looked like old Bohemian and the antiquing of the gilt had become genuine. I figured the women going out the door were averaging twenty carats of diamonds and one hundred pennyweight of gold per minute, not counting platinum and imported junk of various materials. A man at the switchboard hissed my name into the phone and recommended that I go to the ninth floor. I accepted the advice and went into a walnut elevator along with other souls whose varied aura signaled South America, Vienna, and the Near East. My stomach went down to my knees, I got out. Moselle's was Apartment B. The door opened upon a substantial colored woman in a powder-blue uniform who waited for my name and admitted me very politely.

The foyer was scaled to the size of the house, bigger than most living rooms, with doors leading in all directions. The maid opened one and I went through it.

The living room held three large double windows, a thousand books, eight or ten paintings in massive frames, several statues, a big grand piano, two sofas, and maybe a dozen chairs. Mrs. Moselle rose out of one of them when I came in.

"Good evening, Mr. Handy." Her hand was firm. Did I say she was one of those fair brunettes: black hair, black eyes, light skin? Her clear voice matched her handclasp, but with an accent that reminded me somehow of my home town, odd in such a Paris-and-Cannes type. She continued speaking:

"Mr. Moselle has been detained. He will be here in a few minutes. Please sit down."

She motioned toward a chair near the one she had left. We settled ourselves; by turning a little, we faced each other. The maid came in, opened an old-fashioned cellarette, took out a bottle, tray, and glasses, and brought them over to the table which stood between our chairs. She poured drinks into two glasses. There was no bar, and there were no cocktail tables. The lights were low, but not dim, the room unusually quiet; some of those older apartments are almost soundproof. We picked up our glasses and I guessed before I tasted that it was cognac like that I had had in Moselle's office only one night before. – One night! – I sent the brandy down to join the whiskies.

She began, "You've had disagreeable experiences, Mr. Handy."

"Yes," I said. "Very. I don't think I can ever get used to them."

"Let's hope you'll not need to. I suppose the police are satisfied – about that terrible business."

"I'm afraid not."

"They don't think you had anything to do with – " She broke off.

"The body in the car? They just might. It would look better in somebody else's car."

"Ridiculous!"

"I *was* the last man to drive him alive."

We let the silence of the room drift over us. She poured me another brandy and said, "I don't know what Mr. Moselle wants to see you about."

"Neither do I," I replied truthfully. That meant, however, that she knew Moselle wanted to see me; not the other way around. I was observing a pin worn under her throat, a very fine piece. It was gold and had several carats of what I presumed were the best possible stuff, but it was the design that caught my eye – clear, sharp, modern, and unlike anything I had seen. The nearest to it, in feeling, was some ironwork I remembered from Japan and Korea. She knew I was staring, so I said: "I can't take my eyes off that pin, Mrs. Moselle. I think it's the most beautiful thing of its kind I ever saw."

"Thank you." She nodded gracefully. "I always liked it, so I've kept it for myself."

"Kept it?"

"For years now. I never duplicated the design.'

I took this in slowly. "It was made for you, of course."

She seemed surprised. "I made it."

"You design?"

"For more years than I'll tell you. I was Lila Dumont."

It didn't mean a thing to me; I've been in New York only a few years, and I never was in the world of individual pieces. That belongs to Fifth Avenue and Madison Avenue. I didn't think anybody in Moselle's Exchange went into the stuff; there you bring out a design in the morning and several casters have struck it off by four in the afternoon. Forty-seventh Street is strictly C and K – by Carat and by Karat.

"I don't know much about fine pieces." I said. "Did you design for Mr. Moselle?"

"I still do sometimes for the out-of-town trade. We get calls for exceptional things. As Lila Dumont, however, I worked for Battista Bartolomi."

This impressed me. Battista Bartolomi had made a phenomenal success at popularizing fine, handmade Italian jewelry. He had put over the so-called "Florentine finish." By building a following for made-up pieces which were noncompetitive, he avoided the price cutting inseparable from the engagement and wedding ring business. I had never been in his store, but his small shadow-box windows, each holding a group of lovely bracelets, pins, earrings, and necklaces done with precious and semiprecious stones, were a feature of Madison Avenue. He could get more for a turquoise or amethyst ring than Tiffany could get for diamonds. He had branches in various snob resorts about Europe.

I said, "I thought Bartolomi sold only Italian goods."

"Many an Italian piece has been made from my designs. Sometimes all Italy had to do was put on the finish." (Bartolomi's Florentine finish was a sensitive process; not the cheap scratching found on domestic charms and watches.) She went on: "Is Mr. Moselle worried very much about that diamond?" She smiled gravely, looking me in the eye. "I don't like to see him so upset."

I could only say, "I simply don't know, Mrs. Moselle."

I thought it was funny myself, him wanting to see me at his home, but I also wondered why she wondered.

"That's Barney now," she said. We looked at the door; Moselle came through it and up to us, greeting me. He kissed his wife, rather as if he meant it; they had been married five years.

"I'm not so very late, Saul," he said. "Left the store twenty minutes ago."

"Don't you want something to eat, dear?" Lila asked.

"I had a sandwich in the office. Didn't want to keep Mr. Handy too long — let's go into my study. You'll excuse us, Lila."

"Bring Mr. Handy back after you finish. I was enjoying our talk."

I was a hit all around.

Moselle's den was more like an office, complete with a strongbox in the wall which he didn't bother to screen. No doubt he sometimes brought heavy goods home, and Lila must have had plenty. Moselle himself, like most jewelry men, didn't wear a speck of it — not even a tiepin. I can't stand the stuff myself.

60

"So you were a detective, Saul?" This was where we had left off; he was about to lead.

"Oh, yes. I wasn't kidding."

"Didn't you like it?"

"I did. But after Korea I lost the appetite. Didn't need action for a while. I'm a better detective than salesman."

He smiled. "Perhaps a more peaceful one. You're a wild man." He leaned forward, resting his elbows on the desk. "How would you like, Saul, to go back to detecting – as a side line?"

So that was it. I said, "For one thing, I don't have a New York license. But what do you have in mind?"

"Hot diamonds. I don't like them."

"*You* don't like them!"

"I guess you don't either."

"But does this mean, Barney, that you concede the Israeli diamond came from you?"

We looked at each other, and where it counts. His would be a $14,000 answer. The glances held a minute, his face dropped, and he said quite sadly:

"I have found two more stones that are not mine."

Then I knew what it might feel like to come back to life.

"Substituted?"

"How else?"

"Yours are missing?"

"No trace."

I was too pooped to go on. I just sat and watched my hands tremble - it's a funny world. Bender's money had done me more damage than Marder, Cassidy, or Light's dripping corpse. That's this civilization. That's Forty-seventh Street. I said, "Can you give me a sandwich, Barney? I couldn't eat before."

"Good God, Saul! Are you crazy?" He picked up the phone. We sat. The maid came very soon with a tray of sliced bread and cold cuts. "The coffee will be ready in a few minutes," she promised.

"I haven't eaten properly myself," Moselle remarked. "I'm getting old for things like last night. I'm glad I didn't know that Light fellow."

"That's right, you didn't." I was surprised when I

thought about it. "I don't really know him myself – alive that is. I know his carcass."

I was eating now and feeling better with every mouthful. After the coffee, the whole New York underworld was a pushover. I began to make like a cop.

"You must have known this when you saw me this morning, Barney. How did you find time to check your inventory?"

Moselle looked unhappy. "I had already found a substitution before yours came up. I thought it was only a mistake, helped by inexcusable carelessness of my staff and myself. But since you exposed that second one, I went in early this morning and worked on it. By 9:30 I had found the third case."

It doesn't take long to inspect a stock of diamonds – even a big stock. He could pass hundreds under his glass in two hours. Most of it would be routine – obviously the right stone. Only the big ones would matter. Then comes the odd case - first a slight dissatisfaction, then doubt, finally an unwilling acknowledgement.

I asked, "Have you finished the inventory?"

"Yes. There are only three switches."

"You think they were changed while out on memo?"

"How else?"

I didn't answer. There were other ways, such as inside work, but Moselle did so much memo business the other ways could wait. I asked:

"What do you want of me, Barney?"

"I want you to find out how those diamonds are getting into my stock."

"Why me?"

"Do you know anybody could do it better?"

I didn't. There are plenty of detective agencies in New York but which of them could handle this job? He would want it kept confidential and it wouldn't be confidential long if he put a well-known specialist in jewelry crimes on the case. Those guys get results because the underworld knows they can do business with them. But this was no case of compounding a felony under pretense of offering a reward. Whoever had one of Moselle's diamond's didn't need to return it for the reward money; he had paid for it honestly in stolen merchandise of equal value and nobody could say that the goods in his possession weren't his. All you could say was that the goods on Moselle's hands weren't Moselle's. What Moselle needed was a man who could stop his being used as a dumping ground for hot stuff, and stop it without having the publicity put Moselle out of business. It was a sensitive job – top, top secret. I was already in on it, which made me his only no-security risk. By putting me to work, he shut my mouth.

"Have you told Marder?" I asked.

He answered steadily, "Not yet."

"Going to?"

"That's up to you."

"Who knows about this except you?"

"Henry knows about the first one. I had no reason to conceal it."

"The other two?"

"So far only I know. But something must come out sooner or later."

This was more than likely. The newspapers had not mentioned the diamond at all, which meant that Cassidy and Marder were not telling everything they knew. It also meant that they were not sure that I was their man. However, Henry had seen me walk in with the cops.

I asked "How safe are those two stones?"

"In the vault."

"Keep them *very* safe."

"Why?"

"Many reasons. They're evidence. Someone may try to get hold of them again, especially if they're connected to Light's murder. They can be lifted by removing from the vault, by sleight-of-hand stuff over the counter, by a hold-up, and so on."

"How could they be taken out of the vault?"

I looked at him. He sighed. "I guess they could."

"That's why you had me come here. *Never* discount an inside job. How do you want me to work on it?"

"I'm not sure. Are you still with Corbin's?"

"It's a damn good question. So far as I know, I am."

63

"I thought you could do something on the case using Corbin's as a cover."

"Might work. If I come out in the open, I don't think I could accomplish anything. In fact, I'd be a sitting duck. I've already been warned to keep away from police business.

"By whom? Why?" He was disturbed.

"By homicide. However, nobody can keep a man from trying to establish his own innocence."

"The police," he said, "have asked for a list of all memos for larger items given out during the past twelve months."

"How can you do that?"

"I can't, accurately, but I did the best I could. Some of it's memory."

"Marder or Cassidy?"

"Marder."

I liked it one way. At least they were working on other guys. But if I were to try my luck, I would be sniffing over a badly trampled trail. And I didn't like Moselle's spot with respect to the other two stones. He was certainly holding out on them, and if I stuck my nose in, so was I. A cop had been killed over a handful of diamonds. . . .

We had stopped talking; it was time to make up my mind. He had me over a barrel; then again, since he had confided in me, I had him. I still could not have forced him, in court, to return Bender's money; on the other hand, he couldn't afford to be known as a receiver of stolen goods, even by mistake. He must have been reading my mind because his next remark was:

"Call in the morning and I'll refund your money."

I said, "Not yet. Let it keep for a few days."

"Does that mean you're not ready to work on it?"

"It means I'm already working on it." He relaxed. "It would be hard to refund to me without someone getting wise. In fact, I think we'll play it the other way. I'll come in tomorrow and ask for something on memo. Henry will certainly call you. You refuse me. Then I can go all around the market and try out other guys. I want to see what reception I get. – Wait a minute. Give me your police list of everybody who has had a stone over two carats. Ignore small stuff. I particularly want to know about goods returned unsold. Whoever is using you needs an outlet for big stuff which is too hot to sell openly and too good to cut up. Also check your emeralds and stars, value above two thousand."

He was all smiles. "I kept a copy for you," he said, and he gave me a neat handwritten list of about 160 names and addresses arranged in two groups. The larger group consisted of out-of-town accounts

There was nothing more to talk about. We got up together and solemnly shook hands. "See you in the morning," I said. "What are you going to tell Mrs. Moselle?"

"What do you mean?"

"Won't she wonder what I'm doing here?"

"Shouldn't I tell her?" He was frowning.

"Why make her an accessory to withholding evidence? Moreover, it's safer for me this way. She looks like a woman who can keep her mouth shut, but we're all human. Tell her I came to see you about getting my money back, which is the truth. She knows you invited me, so say you wanted to hear my side of it. – Wait. that won't do either. No, tell her I am begging for my money, and that you let me come up here because I must have something to tell Bender tonight."

It was the truth at that. My safest move would be to call Bender at once and tell him I hoped to get the money in a few days. I didn't *think* he would do anything. . . .

Of course, there were some questions right there. Was Bender connected with the jewel racket? The Warrington holdup? Was Light ditto? Light's murder ditto? And why my car?

When I said good night to Mrs. Moselle, she said, "When will we be seeing you again, Mr. Handy?"

I looked at Moselle. He said, "It may be quite soon, Lila. For business reasons, I don't want Saul going in and out of my office right now, and we have some business to finish off. You may be seeing quite a bit of him."

"Mysterious," she said. "I'm glad though. I've enjoyed your visit."

One thing about being raised in a small town: you don't

say "likewise." Going down the elevator, I wondered why she enjoyed my visit.

XIII

No gunman was waiting for me when I slid through the door of my lonely room. I fell into bed; I slept – slept well – and sprang up brightly, come eight o'clock the next morning. I hadn't tried to reach Bender; it couldn't be put off long, but I had decided it could be put off.

So that cool Friday, I sailed into the Corbin Jewelry Company, Manufacturers and Wholesalers, as always, the dapper, energetic, ambitious little producer. Jake Corbin was preoccupied, but not about me. Murray Corbin was tense and worried, but they were his own worries. It was a remarkably steady job. True, I worked cheap for what I did in that joint.

That day I did plenty. The telephone rang steadily; I handled customers, gave advice, took in money, wrote telephone orders, made more decisions than a cabinet minister, and tried to keep potential thieves from cleaning us out. I assured assorted jerks that we had no gambling charms, also no bridesmaids, boxers, St. Bernards, chastity belts, silver charms, gold key chains, or unusual religious items. I took special orders for names cut out of gold disks (*Barbara* the most frequent as usual) and for calendar charms with diamonds set to mark the date the little lovelies were born. Then there were extra-long bracelets for extra-short women, special watches, crazy wedding rings, hideous Florentine pearl earrings, and engraved bangles. – Yes, we will string opera-length pearls, but how long is opera-length? It *could* mean twenty-four inches or more. How many times does your customer want to sling it around her neck? Twenty-four inches will cost one third more than eighteen inches. She doesn't need it so long? More of a

67

musical-comedy length? A G-string length. Figure a dollar an inch above sixteen inches and you won't be far wrong. Yes, a dollar an inch is cheap for some things. For you, it would be a bargain. Yes, *your cost*, a dollar an inch cost to *you*.

–You can approximate the price, can't you? The bracelet has fifteen links, you want two more, that's two fifteenths or one seventh or about 14 per cent. The bracelet is $80 so it may be $11, $12 more. We don't know to the nickel; it depends on how it weighs out. – Yes, you're right, the polishing isn't so good, you can see the file marks; that polisher was really trying to spare our gold. We'll give it a buff. – I don't think the soldering is so good myself; if your customer kicks, we'll make you a new one. – Look, mister, a watch is only supposed to run with reasonable accuracy. It *must* either lose or gain. If it was perfect, there'd be no way to know it because it would be the only thing in the world that *was* perfect, and it would therefore be out of step with every other watch. Don't touch a watch that gains only twenty seconds a day; it will never be so good again. I know you and everybody else has a friend who has a watch that neither loses or gains, but no watchmaker has ever seen one – ... –

Between all this I phoned Moselle and made sure he would be there around 2:00. I arranged with the Corbins to take the afternoon off, beat the dust out of my trouser cuffs, washed my hands in strong detergent to get rid of Corbin's grime – the place looks like a shambles and is as dirty as a lumberyard – and at 1:45 I was admiring Rose's majestic buttocks over a stein of ale.–

She brought me a plate of boiled beef and horseradish sauce for a change. It wasn't a good change.

She said, "I read the papers. Tough for you. Is it over?"

"All over, but the finding of my body. Any news from Bud?"

"Not a word."

"I may get a chance to start asking tonight."

"Oh, that's good! I appreciate it, Saul."

She probably did. She certainly wouldn't want anything

to happen to me until I had found her abstracted expressionist.

I said, "Anybody replace Light yet?"

"I think so. Some of the numbers writers were huddled with a sourpuss I never saw before."

"Any names mentioned?"

"All I know about him is he drinks whisky sours in the morning."

It might be enough to tag the guy by, if I ever needed to. I gave her $1.45 and went back across Sixth Avenue.

The block was in an uproar. Word had got round that someone had made a million-dollar sale and the hungry boys were overwhelmed. Such sales are made once in a while. Every third man seemed to know me, too, but the sale was the big news. I went into Moselle's Exchange and up to his booth. Henry was there.

"Nice sale you didn't get, Henry," I began. "Did they shop you?"

"Weren't in here, Saul. I think they were recommended to Mr. Capple."

Manny Capple was the biggest unindicted gonef in the business. He never would be indicted. He owned two exchanges on the block and had more money than Barney Moselle. His speciality was painting diamonds blue-white. Sometimes an unlucky jeweler did work on one of his gems, put it in acid, boiled it out, and saw it turn yellow under his eyes. Naturally the customer accused the jeweler of switching stones.

I said, "I need a pear-shaped stone, Henry. Very fine color, about three carats."

He never blinked. We looked at several diamonds, and I decided on one already mounted. I said, "Write it up. I'll try to get it back to you tomorrow."

Henry picked up the phone. "Tell Mr. Moselle I need him. Mr. Handy."

We waited quietly for five minutes until Moselle appeared. Solly Myerson came out with him; Solly was an old-timer who could get into the best places. He handled very big stuff.

"Good morning, Saul," Moselle said to me.

Henry handed him the ring. "Mr. Handy wants to take this on memo."

Moselle said, "I can't give you anything, Saul."

I said, "I only want it for the weekend."

He said, "I can't help you."

I said, "I don't pay my bills?"

He said, "I didn't say that."

I said, "I keep the goods out too long?"

He said, "I didn't say that either."

I said, "Drop dead," and walked out of the exchange. I was as red as if he really had turned me down, and I could feel a thousand pairs of eyes boring into me. It would certainly be all over town by tomorrow that Barney Moselle had refused to do business with the guy who had dragged that dead body into Times Square. I was well launched into the case; now all I had to do was solve it.

So, completely discredited in the jewelry business, under suspicion of robbery and murder, what do I do next? I decided to check on Rose's buddy. What the hell – I had an afternoon off, didn't I?

I know an artist; a live artist. I met him by way of a doll picked up in the Metropolitan Museum of Art. A girl alone is a sitting duck in those places; what would she be doing there? A funny thing, too; they always look prettier in a museum; there's nothing like a naked Rubens for making a well-dressed American girl look good. I was already wise to that in Chicago.

This girl knew some cute tricks and she even knew some artists. So one night she took me to a studio party given by a painter named José Quinones, and we – he and I – hit it off pretty good. The girl soon faded back into the bed sheets, but José and I still had a couple of drinks every so often.

I tried his phone, found service had been resumed, found he had never heard of Robert Karl, or Robert Carl even, and arranged to call at his studio around eight o'clock that night and show him my pictures for a change.

So what do I do about my own business? I didn't even have an idea. I went to the Automat on Forty-fifth Street and Sixth Avenue, where there are lots of people with no ideas, and I sat over a cup of coffee and tried to analyze the case.

I could not be sure that somebody was trying to use Moselle for a dumping ground. He did so much business that the three stones *could* have come in by accident. Even if they were planted, it could have been by three different, unrelated parties. Moreover, the diamonds Moselle had turned up were not necessarily stolen. We might never clear up this point. They might remain doubtful items on Moselle's inventory, too hot to handle and too valuable to let go.

If somebody was using Moselle, he was a very smart operator and a big one. He would have to be big to handle such big stuff for the mobs and he must be big to have that much nerve. He would probably be working more than one dealer; not too many in New York – maybe no one else in New York – but say one merchant in each of several large cities. Palming off the stuff would not be too risky; who would be dumb enough to let the police know that their money was inadvertently invested in what might be stolen property? I doubt if the Bank of England is that honest.

If merchandise as dangerous as the Warrington diamonds was being unloaded without recutting, no one man would handle it throughout. If he did, the trail would lead the police to him sooner or later. There had to be second and third parties. Mr. Big would be a very big, secure, prosperous, dangerous man. A man as big as Bender.

I liked Bender as a first suspect. He was in the rackets; he might have made a switch on me and might have planned to unload the hot stone on Moselle using the appraisal as an excuse and me as the patsy. The Israeli diamond might never have been in Moselle's hands at all. Bender would not have expected the appraiser to spot the diamond – who would? Appraisals are the dumbest, dirtiest, cheapest, most ignorant racket in the world. Why the law, the insurance companies, and the trade lets it go on is beyond me. Anybody, anybody at all, can be an appraiser. All you need is a letterhead. Half the appraisals in this city are fixed, the appraiser getting a commission for giving an inflated valuation. Some of the most pretentious stores are mixed up in it. Moreover, most appraisals are made by men who know less than I do, and that's saying plenty.

The way I got that order from Bender was very casual, when I thought about it. I had met him in the street; I had told him where I lived; he had always known me as a jewelry man. One Sunday morning he had called me up, presumably from Crestmere. All very easy, offhand, natural. Maybe too natural.

If Bender was the mastermind, it was his tough luck to hit a capable appraiser with a good memory and an ambition to get in with the police. If Bender was innocent, it was his good luck to have got away from that stone before it sunk him. I doubted if even he could fix a cop murder. It *is* possible, but only if the murder is needed for the protection of the whole system, including the police themselves. *Noblesse oblige* works both ways.

What bothered me was, how the hell could I get at Bender if it was Bender? What could I do that the police couldn't do better?

One good thing: if Bender knew I was only the schmuck who got away, he wouldn't be likely to come gunning for me. The longer I lived the more Bender would look like the man to go after.

What I couldn't find was a connection between Light's murder and Moselle's diamonds. I did not believe Bender to be privy to that; the M.O. was all wrong.

I peered at the list of Moselle's customers. Many of them were well-known business, others were fellows like me, some of whom I knew. Even the police would hardly attempt to check every person connected with each of those businesses. Certainly I couldn't.

There was one thing I could do that the police couldn't. I decided to do it.

I went back to Forty-seventh Street and walked into Number 23A. I knew an old-time diamond trader there, Herman Blok, located on the sixth floor, who used to sell my father some goods. He shared an office with two setters. I went through the outer door, which signaled when I opened it. Inside was a tiny reception room, partitioned to the ceiling like all such places. I rang the bell beside the peepholed window and one of the setters stuck his head out.

"Mr. Blok, please."

"Herman," he yelled, and Herman's face came into focus. I was lucky to have caught him; Blok's business is in his briefcase.

"Hello, Saul, come in." The door leading to the interior opened, and I went past the setters' portion and into Blok's dingy office. The space was eight by ten and held a desk, two chairs, a small, good safe, a filing cabinet, a pair of scales, and a ledger. He could easily do half a million a year with that.

"How you been, boy?" Blok said, enthusiastically pumping my hand. "Haven't seen you in a long time."

"I guess it's a year, Herman."

"What are you doing, boy?"

"I'm still with Corbin's."

"You're there some time now."

"Two years."

"Doing all right?"

He was another tactful one. I said, "Not as well as I should."

He nodded. Blok was about fifty-five, small, slender, gray, and always dressed in gray. He sat at his desk facing me and fingering his diamond tweezers.

"You ought to be able to do better than Corbin's," he remarked. "How can I help you?"

I said, "I'm looking for a side line. I make a deal once in a while using Corbin's merchandise or even Moselle's, but it's not enough. I would like to build something more dependable for myself. I was wondering if you could use a part-time salesman on commission. I could call on some people you don't get around to and occasionally work up a private deal."

"You can do that with Moselle's goods,"

"The price isn't right. I can't make anything. Perhaps you have a few stones you would like to work off, or maybe a finished piece."

He nodded. "I have a couple of things I was going to break up. I bought them right – what I don't see is how you could make out. I have never done enough to support a man."

"At least I could establish myself as a diamond salesman. If it didn't work out, I might then be able to get a regular line of goods. What could you lose?"

"Nothing, but I don't think that either of us could make anything – I heard that Goldenbaum is looking for a man."

"I couldn't get in without a following, and I couldn't afford it if I could. They would only consider a full-time man, and I couldn't work with nothing coming in while I build up a following. What I want is something part-time."

He looked puzzled. He could feel that my proposition was screwy, too silly for me to be serious. He said slowly: "I'll think it over, Saul. I'm not set up to act on the idea today."

I said, "I can understand that. Take a little time on it. I can wait; I'm working. – Herman, could you let me have a good stone or two on memo until Tuesday?"

He gave me a friendly smile. This he could understand; my whole proposition became a build up to get a couple of diamonds out of him.

He said "I guess I can help you out. What size do you need?"

"About two carats, pear-shape."

He went to the safe, pulled out one of the little drawers and took out two papers of goods. He opened them on his desk; each paper held one stone. I examined them, using his tweezers and glass. They were very fine.

"What's the weight?"

"Two-eleven and 2.33."

"How much?"

He pointed with the tweezers. "This is $1,146, and this" (the bigger one) "$1,190."

He meant per carat of course. They were excellent values. I said: "They may be too good but I'd like to try them."

"Price better than Moselle's huh?"

"Yes," I answered truthfully.

"You can't expect him to work so close. He needs that extra 10 per cent."

"Can I keep them until Tuesday?"

"That's O.K."

"How much should I ask for them?"

"You're safe up to $1,450 per carat."

We jawed for two minutes and I left. I caught one of the setters eyeing me as I went out, but there was never a word out of Blok. He certainly could read the papers; he simply was a very nice guy. Even if he learned that Moselle had refused me goods. I doubted that he would cut me off. Of course if the police kept on picking me up, nobody would give me a pushpin.

I didn't know exactly what I was going to do with those diamonds, especially over a weekend. I wanted word to get around that I was trying to sell goods to the trade, so I could call on the people on Moselle's list. Only one of them would know about the stolen diamonds. I would need to be very natural around that one if I was going to learn anything. Or maybe live to learn anything.

I spotted Stony Schultz crossing the street, heading for his shop. He was on the list, he would do for a starter. I followed him into the very old building over one of Capple's exchanges, climbed the stairs to the second floor, and went inside after him.

He had a typical small lapidary shop with a row of cabinets made up of little drawers, each drawer containing a variety of stones, genuine or synthetic, each size of stone wrapped in a marked paper. He could give you a peridot or a topaz of any size from one to perhaps forty centimeters or from one one-hundreth to one hundred carats according to how the particular variety was cut and sold. He had two employees.

His eyes opened wider when he saw me. "How's the morgue, Saul?" he began. He always was a comedian.

I looked at his small head, blotchy face, thin neck, and bony carcass. "Stony, you use diamonds sometimes, don't you?"

"Not much. Once in a while for a customer."

I knew that. He cut a lot of semiprecious stones and

some sapphires, but diamonds are a different business. So I said, "I don't need any. I thought you might want to look at a couple of pears."

"Since when are you a dealer?"

"Herman Blok's goods. I'm carrying a little stuff for him."

"No more Corbin?" (A detestable character.)

I said, "This is a side line."

"I'll take a fast glance."

I opened one paper. If the diamonds got crossed, I would have to weigh them to know which was which. I hadn't had time to really look at them, and I didn't trust my knowledge that far anyhow.

He examined it briefly. "How much?"

It was the bigger one:

"Eleven-fifty."

"Per carat?"

"What do you think?"

He studied it very carefully. The price was too low and he knew it. If he took me up on it, I would have to back out or lose over a hundred dollars. I didn't think he would want diamonds though.

Cautiously he asked, "Have you anything bigger?"

"Not with me. What do you need?"

"Do you have a four-carat emerald cut?"

"This quality?"

"Yes."

"I'll talk to Herman." I folded the paper, almost too quickly.

He said, "So what's with the police, Saul?"

"Nothing."

"No more bodies?"

"Not yet. You never can tell."

"Ha-ha-ha. You never can tell, Saul, can you? You never can tell."

I didn't hit the miserable runt. "How soon do you need the emerald-cut?"

"Who needs it? If you have one, I'll look at it."

I left. I couldn't bring myself to shake hands. I had done what I wanted to do; the old drip would get word all over the street that I was peddling diamonds and that they were very, very cheap. It was bait; I might get a nibble.

On the landing at the top of the stairs I passed a man who hardly belonged, a most correctly dressed man even to a Homburg hat; tall, slender, with the carriage of an athlete, about forty-five, and he looked like a man who called the signals. He went through Schultz's door. I didn't know him; if he was a jewelry man, he wasn't in my world. He might have been an amateur stone collector, probably from Buenos Aires.

I still had time for one more. I went into Capple's Exchange and up to his booth. I didn't know the salesman.

"I would like to take out an emerald-cut, around four carats, very fine color, on memo. I'm Saul Handy – Corbin Jewelry Company."

"Do you want it for your company?"

"No, for myself."

"I guess we can take care of you."

We looked at merchandise for twenty minutes. He promised to locate what I wanted by Monday noon. I left a specimen of my signature and showed identification. If they gave it to me Monday, it meant that Moselle's refusal hadn't cut me off.

There wasn't much time left to that day, so I went back to Corbin's, put Blok's diamonds in the safe, and pulled the stock. We were ready to give the signal when Harry Abner knocked on the door, which of course, since we were closed, was bolted on the inside.

Abner was a typical diamond setter who did some work for Corbin's. Like most diamond setters he dressed well, worked in his good clothes, had an excellent income, and a certain refinement of speech and manner. Diamond setters are the aristocrats of the business. He was about fifty years old.

The jewelry business abounds in obscene merchandise. Rings and pins illustrating every conceivable form of sexual activity are as common as phallic images in a biblical digging. No ringmaker is too lousy a workman to turn these out as a side line, and they never seem to get tired of doing them.

We had let Abner in and taken some of our work from him when he opened a shopping bag.

"Would you like to see the newest in work aprons?" he asked in his rather finicky tones.

The Corbins, the porter, and I gathered around him. He took out an ordinary short blue denim apron, such as jewelers and other workmen use, and put it on, his graying head looming satyrlike above it. The apron had three unusual features: three zippers running up and down, one on each side and one in the middle. The left zipper was neatly embroidered "Hers," the right one "His," and the center one "Mine".

"His," he called dramatically, ran the zipper down, and six inches of his sprang out. "Hers," he announced, and hers, artistically constructed out of suitable materials, came suddenly into view.

"Would you like to see mine?"

We would. The center zipper slid down and "mine" appeared, very lifelike, modest in girth and rather limp, but a foot long.

And there stood that graying gentleman, the apron and its ornaments set against his dignified gray suit, and the four spectators, of whom I was the youngest, bent in convulsions around him like pagans at a fertility rite.

We closed. I ate spaghetti at Johnnie's, and after killing as much time as I could, I set out for Quinones' studio.

It was in an East Side loft building, less than a mile from Corbin's. The police still had my car. I had time, so I walked. Nobody followed me that I could see; if the police had a tail on me, he was good at it. I hoped they had; it would be protection if Bender got ideas.

Quinones had a party in full swing when I got there; he served beer and the guests spiked it with whatever they had brought. Quinones is a pretty good painter in a half-modern manner: you can make out what he has painted, but not why. The studio was big. The chairs were boxes topped with planks, the walls were well covered with his pictures and also some of his friends' masterpieces.

José is very Spanish. When he wears slacks and shirt, he

looks like somebody training to be a bullfighter; tonight, in a smock, more like a Mexican chef.

There were fifteen or twenty people; the unshaded lights were ghastly; but the crowd seemed to be having a good time. None of them staggered. It was mostly new to me. I liked it though, once in a while.

José said, "People, this is Saul Handy."

Several looked closely at me; I had become a personality. I knew a few of them; I shook hands a couple of times and picked up a glass, to look natural. I was too full of spaghetti and red wine to start on beer.

In a few minutes José came over to me. "You wanted to show me something, Saul?"

"Did you ever see this guy?" I showed him Karl's picture.

"Yes." He looked at me curiously.

"Where does he live?"

"Isn't he in the phone book?"

"No."

"That's funny. He certainly can afford a phone."

"He does pretty good?"

"All those guys are doing pretty good.- Hey, does anybody know where Raphael D'Arle lives?"

Two did. His studio could have been seen from the doorway of the White Lily – New York is a funny town.

Quinones and I walked to one side.

"So its D'Arle. I had Karl. What do you know about him, José?"

"Has he murdered anybody?"

I winced. "You too. He doesn't even owe me money."

"Not right now."

"He wouldn't be cheap."

"I get my picture taken for nothing."

"Believe me, a portait by him is different."

"My worst enemy wouldn't know me. Is he married?"

"Not that I ever heard – with his clientele, it's better single."

"Is he any good – as a painter?"

"For all I can tell," José said ernestly, "he's as good as Pollock. If Pollock can paint, he can paint.

79

"He's not making that kind of money, is he?"

"Not yet. But he might. If he doesn't get married. He's a smart cookie."

I was watching the back of a woman dressed in dark red. It was a good back, and from where I stood it was draped more for D'Arle's studio than for Quinones'. She was concentrating fiercely over one of José's paintings, which stood on an easel in the middle of the floor. When she turned to me, I was too surprised to speak.

Lila Moselle was not surprised at all. She stood by the bright green painting in slender scarlet, with a large, odd, gold shoulder pin from which came the gleams of emerald. A heavy bangle around her slim arm gave the same regal glints. Her black hair and eyes were startling amidst that red, green and gold. I would never see a more beautiful woman.

"You didn't tell me, Mr. Handy, that you pursued the Arts." As I came nearer, she held out her hand. It, too, bore a heavy emerald.

I answered slowly, "You did tell me."

"You know each other?" Quinones said.

"We frequently meet," she said suavely.

"And in many different situations," I added.

"Excuse me," José said, leaving us as three badly dressed guests came in.

"This situation," said Lila, "is a pleasant one,"

"I thought our last was."

She was looking into my face pleasantly enough. She didn't look any older than I did and for the first time it occured to me that Moselle might be too old for her.

She said, "I overheard José asking about Raphael D'Arle."

"Yes, I wanted his address."

"He has a phone."

"I looked in the wrong place."

"Like José, I am intrigued by your interest. Do you go in for abstract art?"

"Not when I can help it. Do you know Mr. D'Arle?"

"We've met. When I worked I had to keep in touch with

this kind of thing. I got to know quite a few artists in this town."

"You were not born in New York, I take it,"

"Is anybody?" She pointed to a plank resting on two boxes. "Let's sit a minute."

After I carefully came down beside her, she moved a little closer. "Anything new?"

"About me? No, I haven't talked to a policeman in twenty-four hours."

"I thought perhaps something about Barney."

"Not by me." So Moselle had told her.

She waited for a minute while I said nothing, and then she said, "So why are you interested in Raphael?"

"A third party is the interested one. I'm only getting information."

"You sound like a detective."

"I used to be."

"I know." She was inspecting my face thoughtfully. "We must see more of each other, Mr. Handy. I'm going to ask you to cocktails. Can you get off a little early on a week-day?"

"I can always tell the boss I'm wanted for questioning."

I thought her eye flashed, but you can go way off eye flashes. I asked, "Do you know Robert Karl?"

She barely hesitated. "That's the name you had for Raphael, isn't it?"

She hadn't missed much. "Yes," I answered. "Ever hear it before?"

"Not that I remember."

I felt she had a good memory. There was no use my hanging around José's so I said something to her and to José and left – I hadn't even tasted the beer.

I walked all the way back with one eye over my shoulder and ended up on the Forty-seventh Street block. The windows were dark now; all doors were sealed. The two bookstores and the thrift shop were black. Only the avenues were alive: Madison soft and rich, Fifth spacious and arrogant, Sixth greasy and squirming. The White Lily was open but Rose wouldn't be there, and those places are more repulsive after dark. So I walked to my third-rate hotel, tried TV, gave up, and went to bed. A tiring day and a poor one.

XIV

As soon as I got out of bed on Saturday I knew I was going to have a good day. It was nine o'clock. I took a shower, put on my best suit, and walked for fifteen minutes before breakfast. Then, to show how tough I felt, I went to a phone booth and got homicide on the wire. Sergeant Cassidy accepted my call.

"Decided to come clean, Handy?"

"I want my car, and don't tell me you're not through with it."

"We're not through with it."

"What are you doing? Renting it out for the benefit of the P.B.A.?"

"What do you need it for? Going some place?"

"Only to my lawyer."

"Be sure he's a good one." He hung up.

What lawyer? I asked myself. I didn't even have a doctor.

I walked over to Forty-seventh Street. It was busy already with retail customers, but of course you can't talk to buyers on Saturday even if you're not really selling anything. I went along the south side to Fifth Avenue, kept on going to Madison and turned north until I reached Battista Bartolomi's sniffing store front, where I admired some superb beads of coral and turquoise with a clasp of diamonds and gold that reminded me of Lila Moselle's pin. I wondered how I was going to get in there with my line of diamond bargains. It was on Moselle's list.

Then I walked back, along the north side of Forty-seventh Street, said hello twice, passed Corbin's locked door (we have no windows), looked into Moselle's Exchange, and watched Henry and at least six other men showing goods and talking like crazy. I went two blocks down Sixth Avenue and into a crummy doorway below the studio of a rising New York abstract expressionist.

The stairway stank as bad as Schultz's place. There was no name downstairs, not even on the mailbox, but he did have his name on a third-floor doorway. I knocked (no bell either) and wondered what I was going to say. The idea was to help Rose.

Somebody shuffled to the door after a while, and it opened on a man: tall, disorderly, in a bathrobe and bare feet, very sullen, blond, and very handsome. I saw what Rose saw in him; he resembled the snapshot close enough to tell me that the rest was up to her.

"Am I too early to come in, Mr. D'Arle?" I began, in my smoothest salesman's voice.

He was trying to make like a salesman too. "Not at all. I did oversleep, Mr.–?"

"Handy. Saul Handy." I held out my hand; he took it.

"I'll have to dress a little. Can you give me five minutes?"

We were inside a large studio which led to at least one other room. He evidently had the whole floor. I saw paintings all about; the effect was cheerful in morning light. D'Arle was studying me covertly, which was natural enough.

I said, "Don't let me be any trouble, Mr. D'Arle. I want to look at your work."

"Just five minutes."

So I stood alone in a wide acreage of colored canvas, none of which said a thing to me except just that. Some of it was painted, some was dribbled, some was pasted, but none of it talked. The prize for uselessness went to six or eight big jobs consisting of one broad loud color, four feet by eight, and two bordering stripes, one by eight, running from floor to ceiling. What the hell would you do with them? They looked like colored sketches of stage draperies for a poorhouse theatrical.

Then there were things made by pasting all kinds of objects on to a big board, such as an old garage door. One of these featured a cotton sock in the foreground. The masterpieces looked like a portion of a badly littered courtyard in East Harlem. I knew this was what people were buying and I wondered what I was going to say to D'Arle about it.

Before I had found the answer he came back, in a sport shirt, slacks and loafers. He was a very big guy.

I didn't like his face. He would affect the women; there was a lot of animal in him and a smoothness with it, but there was also something rancid. Maybe it was his pictures, which suggested to me, more and more, a design for decorating the main hall of the garbagemen's union.

"And what can I do for you, Mr. Handy?"

I had to say something. I didn't think I could fool him for a minute if I posed as a picture buyer. My job was done; I couldn't tell him to do the right thing by Rose, especially since I couldn't imagine what the right thing would be with this character. The trick was to get out without doing any harm.

I said, "You know José Quinones?"

"Certainly. I have known José for years. (This quite deadpan.)

"He told me to look at your work."

"He did?" He was neither surprised nor particularly amiable. Just noncommittal. He must have known that Quinones was not an unrestrained admirer of his art, but I was counting on natural vanity.

"Yes," I said. "He thought I could get a good idea from your pictures of what abstract painting is about."

"That was kind of him." I decided that he meant this for a friendly remark. "When," he went on, "did you discuss me?"

"Only last night," I assured him.

"You acted promptly."

"Today was my best opportunity. I wanted to look in daylight."

"Fortunate it didn't rain." (This might have been said dryly, but I didn't know him well enough to be sure.)

"Do you collect paintings, Mr. Handy?"

"Collect is too strong." And now I had a moment of inspiration. "I'm a jewelry man, Mr. D'Arle, and my interest stems from that."

"You design?" (Was he kidding me?)

"I wish I could."

"It's an expensive branch of collecting," he said slowly.

"Not necessarily. I don't go in for emeralds."

"Nor diamonds, I suppose." Now I knew something was wrong.

"Have you heard of me, Mr. D'Arle?"

"You're a famous man, Mr. Handy."

The only thing to do was play it naïve. I said, "I hope you haven't let the newspapers prejudice you against me."

"Why should I?"

"No reason. I'm absolutely harmless, only unlucky."

"Crime splashed on you as it went by."

"That's about it."

"Still it's not too surprising."

"What do you mean?"

"Aren't you a detective?"

He *could* have got all this from the papers. I didn't see any paper around the studio. I didn't know how many artists read crime news. Light's case hadn't been played up much in those papers which play up art shows. Still, I *had* been recognized at Jośe's party. . . .

I said, "I was on the Chicago police for a time – years ago."

"And now you came up to look at my etchings."

It was time to get out. I didn't want a thing from the guy; I needn't have come except to verify his face before raising Rose's flowers of hope. So I said:

"Would you be willing to explain to me some of your ideas? That's how Jośe and I came to talk about you. I don't understand modern art."

"Couldn't Jośe enlighten you?" This was a sneer; I couldn't blame him. He knew I was a phony intruding on his privacy and all that. Still, there was something wrong with the interview.

I said cautiously, "I don't think Jośe claims to understand abstract art either. For instance, Mr. D'Arle, what does that sock mean?"

I thought he would tell me it meant the death of a flatfoot, but he managed a smile, a stale smile, and launched into a lecture about the expression of the artist's pure moods. I yessed him along, working toward the door. Finally to keep up the pretense, if you could call it that, I said:

"Do you design jewelry?"

His eyes and mouth changed only a little, but it was enough to make him look like a poor future for Rose.

"No."

"That's what I was really interested in, Mr. D'Arle. I'll go now. It's been a pleasure meeting you and your talk was very instructive."

"I've enjoyed your visit," he said grimly. "Thank José for sending you."

"We'll talk about you over our beers."

And now, perhaps because his lecture had stimulated my usually inactive mind, I remembered something. I saw it, sharp and strong, clearer than when it was in front of me. "Mr. D'Arle, is that modern painting in Mr. Bender's library by you?"

"You know Helene Bender?" He was really trying to read me.

"I've met her."

"They have two of my pictures." Something about me had him guessing.

We shook hands. He held the door for me. I held my breath and went down the two flights of stairs.

The Avenue of the Americas did no more for Sixth Avenue than Raphael D'Arle did for Robert Karl. I wondered which was his real name – not that it was going to matter to Rose. He was one stone dead end, so far as I could see.

I thought about his changing moods as I had mentioned my name, Quinones, jewelry designing, and Bender. Funny that he should know all the women in my life at the moment: Rose, Lila, Helene.

The good mood of the morning was over. I could have used a mouthwash. It was early for a drink, so I went back to my hotel. The desk man, an uninviting lush called Bernie, signaled me.

"Those men are waiting for you. I think they're policemen."

Cassidy and his valet were squatted in two of the shabby chairs which decorated the lobby. I looked at Bernie's malicious mouth and said, "That's your trouble; you try to think with it. Use it sometimes for what it's good for."

And to the seated public servants. "Did you bring my car?"

Cassidy got up reluctantly. "We want to talk to you."

"Anywhere in particular?"

He looked at the other member of the badly balanced team. "Do you think his suite is ready to receive us?"

The straight man answered, "Ours is if his isn't"

"This way," I said contemptuously, and went to the elevator.

I live on the seventh floor. As I unlocked the door, I said, "Don't spit on the carpet if the chambermaid's inside. She's from a refined family."

I took the only chair and let them sit on the bed. Cassidy looked hard at me.

"You're still in the diamond business."

"I left the only business they pay you for doing nothing in when I left Chicago."

"Where did you get those diamonds?"

"The Tiffany robbery. Remember: when the cops took a walk and let the crooks trim the windows?"

Partner said, "Let's take this punk downtown."

Cassidy said, "Don't you think it's a legitimate question, of a man who handles stolen goods?"

"If you know so much you know damn well where I got the goods."

"You didn't get them from Moselle. If you want, we can ask around town until we find out."

I didn't want, so I said, "Herman Blok, if it's any of your business. You're supposed to work on homicide cases."

Cassidy turned to Partner. "Knows police work. Sharp as a whip. – What's Blok's address?"

I told him. "Try not to give him the idea he shouldn't trust me with merchandise."

"Should he?" asked Partner.

Cassidy said, "You can get your car."

I said, "Would it be asking too much to ask you to bring it uptown?"

"No. But if you don't want a garage bill, get it out by Monday." He got up and stretched himself. "Do you own a gun?"

"Yes," I said, "I have a permit." They knew this well enough, since I had the permit on me when they searched me at headquarters.

"Let's see it."

"What for?"

He didn't answer. I took it out of my dresser drawer and handed it to him. It wasn't loaded and hadn't been fired in years. Cassidy examined the side of the barrel carefully, wrapped it in a handkerchief, and put it in his pocket.

"What's that for? Light wasn't shot."

"How right you are. He was clubbed with something hard."

"So where was it when you picked me up?"

"Sharp as a whip. – You don't carry a gun?"

"Not ordinarily."

"Don't."

"Why?"

"I don't want one on you."

"Then revoke the permit. Until then I'll do as I please."

"Whichever way you want it."

They left. I stood looking at the door, trying not to kick it.

XV

I didn't know what more I could do on a Saturday. None of the names on Moselle's list gave me ideas, although Stony Schultz was capable of cooking his grandmother for a small commission and Capple, the diamond painter, was an absolute crook. However, he was almost too rich and too old for this stuff. Certain fine houses, such as Wise Brothers in Cleveland and Donahue in Boston, were too snobbish to be serious suspects and too far away for me to investigate. Bartolomi was beyond suspicion, although I could walk over there for the hell of it. The remaining names were pure leg work.

I picked up the phone and called Moselle's office. Mr. Moselle had not come in that day, very unusual for him. I tried his home.

The maid answered, "Moselle's residence."

"Mr. Moselle, please."

"Who is calling?"

"Mr. Handy."

"One moment, please."

Then another woman's voice came through, and I knew this one.

"How are you, Mr. Handy?"

"Art-sick, but still able to go on."

"You sound as though your interest in art was rather sudden."

"Sodden, rather."

She hesitated. "What can I do for you?"

"I would like to talk to Mr. Moselle."

"I try to keep Barney away from business over the

weekend. He is excessively tired. Can't I help you? Take a message?"

"It's of some importance to me."

A pause: "I'll call him."

Presently Barney's voice: "Yes, Saul."

"Barney, I want you to pick me out some merchandise. One stone, if possible, in the three-carat range, and one emerald-cut, four carats. Give me the rock-bottom wholesale – your cost. The emerald-cut should not go above $1,400 per carat. Also, give me those two substituted diamonds. Keep very exact descriptions of all the goods. Get them to me in such a way that no one – but no one – will know it."

"When do you want this?"

"Not later than Sunday morning, unless you are too sick to attend to it. I'm going to have them microscopically photographed."

"Bait?" he said softly.

"Yes."

"Suppose the stones *are* hot and the police find them on you?"

"You will cover me."

"And go to jail myself?"

"Do you *know* they're hot?"

"Of course not!"

"That's the point. Can you bring them to my hotel?"

"I guess so. I'm tired. About when?"

"When you're ready. Leave a message at the desk to phone Mr. Richards. In case you are going any place, give me phone numbers and times. I'll call you."

"Can do. I'm not going anywhere. . . . I hope you know what you're doing."

"So do I."

So now what? I consulted my wallet and called a number in a very rich Westchester town. A woman's voice answered; a maid, no doubt.

"The Bender residence."

"Mr. Bender, please."

"Who is calling, please?"

"Mr. Handy."

"Just a minute, Mr. Handy."

Another woman's voice came through, and I recognized this one too, although I had heard it only once.

"This is Mrs. Bender."

"How do you do, Mrs. Bender. Can I talk to your husband?"

"He's not at home."

"Can you give me a number so I can reach him?"

"What do you want, Mr. Handy?"

"I want to talk business."

"Mr. Bender has already talked business with you."

"Yes, Mrs. Bender, and it was a bad business. I'm very sorry, especially sorry that you could not have had the enjoyment from that diamond that he meant you to have. But I really do need to talk to him."

"I'll see if I can reach him. Where can he call you?"

I gave my hotel number. Her thanks sounded like glass breaking under intense cold. I couldn't blame her; I wasn't her type of salesman. Her voice, I realized, although as smooth as Lila Moselle's, was different. It was New York, say Brooklyn, via Vassar, whereas Lila reminded me of my home town. Suddenly I remembered that D'Arle also talked like a Westerner – an arty Westerner – say Des Moines via Evanston.

I sat for twenty minutes and looked at the peeling wallpaper. I thought I should get a little apartment farther uptown – unfurnished maybe – and make a place for myself that wouldn't look like nobody was home. Or get married. The Corbins had a baby sister who had never married and was under thirty. She used to help out during the Christmas rush.

The phone rang. A voice, which could have been Al Light's, said:

"Handy?"

I conceded the point.

"Hold on."

Then a very crisp tone: "This is Bender."

I took a breath. "Ed, I want to talk to you."

"What about?"

"Your money."

92

"What's there to talk about?"

"I think I can give it to you in a few days."

"Mail me a check – a banker's check."

"I want to talk to you first."

A slight pause. "When?"

"Now, if possible."

"I'll be in my office for the next hour."

"What's the address?"

He gave it to me. It was a large office building less than ten minutes' walk from my hotel.

"I'll be there in fifteen minutes." I said. I grabbed my hat and headed for the street. After six minutes of fast walking I reached Bender's address, went to a phone booth in the lobby, dialed police headquarters and asked for Lieutenant Marder. He was out.

"Will you give him this message as soon as possible? Tell him Saul Handy is going into Ed Bender's office to talk business pertaining to a certain sum of money. Tell him I am not armed. I will call him again in not more than two hours. If I do not call, he should notify Sergeant Cassidy and investigate. I do not expect trouble."

I gave my address, and Bender's, and hung up before the man could figure out a stall while he sent out an order to pick me up. There was no reason to, but God only knows what a desk man will do. I went over to the uniformed elevator starter, a thin individual with a mouth like Bernie's at my hotel, and gave him my card and a folded dollar bill.

"I am going to the sixteenth floor, room thirty-four, to see Mr. Bender. He expects me. You may get an inquiry for me before I come down. If so, please send the party to Mr. Bender's office." I stepped into the next elevator going up before he could answer.

Room 34 was only one door away. I wondered how many of the businesses marked on the other doors were Bender enterprises. My hand faltered for a moment before it turned the knob, but I remembered I used to be a cop.

The reception room was small, but very fancy and equipped with a standard blonde. In another mood I would have tried something for size, but the way I felt, I gave my name and told her Mr. Bender was expecting me.

She gave it into the phone and I could estimate the quality of my welcome since she said, "Just a minute," without asking me to sit down.

It only was a minute. A man came out, dressed in a black business suit, and held the door for me. It wasn't courtesy that made him stand aside, and it wasn't innocence that kept him from frisking me after he had closed the door behind us. He simply wasn't the kind who went through doors first, and he wasn't the kind who needed to frisk anybody. The only thing he did was stay close.

The door led to an interior-partitioned corridor. The corridor had a number of doors. He motioned me along from a position slightly back of me until we had passed four of them. Then he rang a bell. A signal buzzed, like a door to a diamond dealer's place, and I preceded him into a sensibly furnished executive's office. Bender's desk faced the door and he was facing me as I came in.

"What do you want?"

"May I sit down?"

"Why?"

I began to lose my temper. "Because I can kick better sitting down." I dropped into a chair at the edge of his desk. "I think I can get Moselle to refund the money by the end of next week."

"Why should he do that?"

"He concedes that it may be his responsibility."

"Expensive concession." he said. I could not detect from his face that he knew anything he hadn't known the last time I saw him. He resumed, "What do you want of me?"

"Information?"

"Like?"

"Al Light."

He gave me the fish eye until his phone rang. He answered it, gave rapid instructions, which might as well have been in code and which may have been gambling data, and hung up. Light's name certainly had not disturbed him. I was reasonably sure he was clear on the murder, but I didn't know whether he thought I was or not. Finally he said:

"You can only kill him once," It didn't have much conviction, just a rib, and I felt relieved.

I said, "You know I didn't have anything to do with that."

His face darkened. "What do you mean 'know'?"

I hadn't meant a thing, but I took the opening. "Who would know better?"

He looked very ugly but at that moment the phone rang again. This time it wasn't gambling business.

"Yes . . . yes . . . Why? . . . No idea of it. . . . Certainly plays it safe. . . . Absolutely not. O.K., lieutenant." He held the phone out to me with a sneer. "Your protection wants to talk to you."

It was Marder. "What the hell are you doing there?" he began.

"I owe the man money. Don't you remember?"

"You're in no position to play cute, Handy." How they love to put that in. "What are you up to?"

"Nothing at all. I spoke to Sergeant Cassidy only an hour ago."

"Did you help him as much as you've helped me?"

"I am always co-operative."

"Be careful, Handy. Don't get killed before we can close the case on you."

"The case or the jaws?"

"It'll probably come to the same thing." He hung up.

Bender looked up at his soldier for the first time. "This guy was no hero, even in Korea [Bender almost was]. He's strictly a rear-echelon man." The bodyguard laughed briefly.

The time had come to get serious. I said, "Bender, do you think I had anything to do with Light's murder?"

"To tell you the truth," he answered quietly, "I can't see you to take him. Al had to be surprised. You couldn't have surprised him; he was laying for you. You could never have killed him, that way, after he surprised you – not Al Light. Either there were two in on it, or it was somebody he trusted."

It was a professional judgment; he knew me. I said , "I

95

figure that's the way the police see it. Now, back to the big one. What do you know about the murder?"

"Is that what's worrying the police?"

I thought he was covering a trace of worry himself, so I said, "I get that idea."

"Why me?"

"Because he tried to palm the hot diamond off on you."

"And then went to an appraiser and got himself picked up?"

"Could have been a smart move. It was ten thousand to one against the appraiser's recognizing the diamond. When he did, Light had a perfect cover – me."

"If Light slipped the hot diamond in, where is the right one? And why would Moselle feel responsible?"

"If Light switched stones, the right one could be anywhere. Most likely, he gave it to a confederate. However, since Moselle knows he didn't wrap up the diamond he meant to give me, he may have handed out the Warrington stone."

It was as much information as I intended to give him. He got up, went to a small safe, came back, and laid down a little white paper. When he opened it, a big diamond blinked gaily. And it was a pear-shape.

"What do you think of this stone?"

I scanned his face, took out my glass, picked up the paper, and examined the diamond as well as I could without tweezers. He had fluorescent lights, which didn't help. It was a fair stone, about the same size as the Israeli diamond, but not nearly so fine. I couldn't see any obvious defects, and it was technically white, but it had no fire, beauty, life.

I said, "Are you going to buy it?"

"What's it worth?"

"I'm not a fully qualified diamond buyer, but it's way below the goods I showed you. What's the weight?"

"How should I know?"

I put the paper down. "Is this a hot stone?"

"I don't know that either."

"Where did you get it?"

"Light had it."

96

My brain spun. "Was he trying to sell it to you?"

"I think he was planning to pass it off on me."

I took this in slowly. I had said it first but I hadn't meant it. "You mean he was first going to get an appraisal based on my diamond, and then give you this one. It probably would have worked. But then he couldn't have made the first switch; in fact, he was just as surprised as he seemed to be. Wait a minute – why didn't the police find this stone on him?"

"I suppose they didn't search him. Why should they? He was only running an errand for me. Maybe it wasn't on him when they picked him up."

"Was it on him when he was killed?"

He looked at the guard and jerked his head toward me. "Always the cutie."

"How *did* you get hold of it?"

"It was in his apartment."

I didn't bother to ask him how he got there ahead of the police. He probably knew that Light had been murdered five minutes after the word reached homicide. His first move would be to check Light's home, wherever that was, for anything he might not want publicized.

I asked, "What are you going to do with it?"

"What's it worth?"

"Not over five thousand. You can't give it to Mrs. Bender."

He said bitterly, "What the hell will I do with it?"

"Even if it wasn't stolen?"

"Even if it wasn't stolen."

"Even if it wasn't stolen, it is now. You might give it to the police."

"I might." He picked up the paper and put it on his desk. "I'll decide that. I don't want the police asking for it before I'm ready to give it to them."

"They won't because of me."

He looked at the third man. "You heard him, Wally? They won't ask for it because of anything he says."

"I heard him."

"Don't forget it."

A tough look or speech would have been wasted on

Wally. Instead I said, "Do you know where Light's car was parked last night?"

"In the same lot."

It added up. Bender hadn't had time nor reason to kill Light but he was a bit tarnished by the whole business – made a little more vulnerable, and that in a line of work where vulnerability is expensive. It was clear that Light had been waiting for me in my car, and had been completely surprised. But who would even know he was in there, never mind surprise him? I liked my position, as against Bender, better and better.

It was time to get something out of this talk. I said, "What do you know about Al Light?"

"He worked for me."

"Long time?"

"Six, seven years."

"Good man?"

"Very."

I didn't ask for what, "Police record?"

"Something way back."

"What for?"

"Assault or like that."

"Armed robbery?"

"I'm not sure."

"Where?"

"Out west."

"Chicago?"

"Somewhere further."

"Was he a real Westerner?"

"Italian or part Italian."

"There aren't so many Italians between Iowa and California."

"He was."

"Do you know his Italian name?"

"No."

"Do you know of any woman who might be involved in the murder?"

This surprised him. "Hell, no. Who?"

"The police have an idea."

"I don't know much about his women," he said thoughtfully.

All this had amounted to exactly nothing. "You can't think of a thing that would help find his killer or the source of the hot merchandise?"

"No."

"Or you won't?"

He didn't get mad. "As a matter of fact, Saul," he said quietly, "I would."

"Me, but not the police?"

"Maybe not the police."

"Why the honor?"

"What the police are really interested in is the Warrington job, which is no skin off me. But Light was one of my boys. I would like to know what happened and who."

"Does that mean you're not laying for me?"

He looked at me distastefully. "Let's keep something straight: I want my money."

"You'll get it," I hoped.

He went on. "We don't have one thing on Light. He may have planned to chisel on me or he may not. It's only talk. But you took my money and I ended up with the stolen goods. I'm not holding the bag."

He stopped. I said nothing, so he said, "That's all I have against you. If I get my money, we're still friends, even though your damned diamond put a fire under me."

"The police bothering you?"

"Not the police, wise guy. My wife."

I said, "I'm really sorry about that. I wanted Mrs. Bender to enjoy that beautiful stone. She sounded chilly over the phone."

"Did she know Al Light?"

"What do you mean, know?"

He laughed. "Helene is very loyal."

"Did she ever meet him?"

"What's it to you?"

"If she thinks I had anything to do with the murder, it wouldn't make her think more of me."

"I guess it wouldn't."

"Would she like to hear I was fished out of the East River?"

"Hard to say."

I got up. "O.K., Ed. You'll hear from me next week."

"I want to."

We didn't shake hands. The escort went with me to the reception room and then stood in the doorway until I went through the outer door. The blonde didn't look up. I didn't look back.

When I reached the lobby, I asked the starter, "Anybody ask for me?"

"No, sir."

I went to the phone booth and got Marder. He began, "What did you want with Bender?"

"Information."

"Like what?"

"Like Light had a police record out west. If not his own name, then maybe it's an Italian name."

A brief pause. "Where out west?"

"I don't know. West of Chicago."

"What else that you haven't told the police?"

"Light was a very tough man. He had to be killed by someone he trusted."

"Bender told you that?"

"Yes."

"Have you told homicide?"

"I'll let you do it."

"Don't push homicide, Handy. They're not the ones to take it."

"Who's pushing?"

"Cassidy will probably thank you in person."

He hung up. I left the booth and moved slowly toward the door. I was trying to see a pattern in what I had learned. I was tired; why, I didn't know. I had taken D'Arle, Cassidy and Bender in four hours, but nobody had done anything to me. The combination simply didn't sit well on my stomach.

A tonic was waiting for me as I went into the street. A tall, sumptuous woman, dressed like a dream and arrogantly gracious, almost collided with me.

"I fear," I said, "the pleasure is all mine."

No reply.

"You made very good time, Mrs. Bender. You must have been ready to leave when I spoke to you."

No answer.

"Mrs. Bender, there is something I would like to ask you." This drew a glance that was all arrogance, the arrogance heightened by an odd scratch over one eye. "I have learned that you are acquainted with Raphael D'Arle. In fact you have some of his paintings. Do you know him well?"

She answered quietly. "I do not see, Mr. Handy, that the range of my acquaintance is any concern of yours."

"It is," I assured her. "Everything about you and Mr. Bender is now my concern. For example, did you know D'Arle as well as you knew Al Light?"

Her face went from arrogance to bewilderment to anger. "Good day, Mr. Handy" she said in clipped tones and swept into the lobby. The conversation had not been a success.

I took six steps, stopped dead, turned, and stared at the granite entrance. That regal perfume . . .

Forty-seventh Street looked the same when I got back to it. I wasn't hungry myself but I needed a change, so I went into the Wentworth Bar and had a couple of bourbons. Then I ate veal parmigiano with spaghetti, in memory, I guess, of Al Light. What the hell; it was too late for flowers.

XVI

It was twelve noon on Sunday before I heard from Moselle. He arrived at my hotel fifteen minutes after his phone call. I felt a little ashamed of my crumby room. He looked around for a second chair; I sat on the bed and admired his handsome gray head. He was carefully dressed, and not by Howard.

I took the envelope he offered me. "Four diamonds," he said. "One mounted. Two are suspect. Anything come up?"

"I saw Bender yesterday."

He was startled. "And?"

"Light has a criminal record. It isn't his name either. I told the police."

He nodded. "I'd watch myself. What else?"

I told him about Herman Blok. Then he said, "By the way, be careful with those stones. I'm not sure the insurance company would pay me if they were lost."

"Why?"

"There's a clause to the effect that anyone guilty of a suspicious act must not be entrusted with merchandise. For instance, an employee must be discharged immediately and not re-hired until he is cleared."

"I'm not an employee."

"I know that. I'm listing the stones as my personal property and covering them with my own floater, but I'm still not sure they would pay off."

I shrugged. I didn't intend to lose the diamonds, but it was his idea that I should work on it. We got up and went out; he took a cab to his home. I went along with him to Fifty-eighth Street.

One of the best gemologists in the city lived on that

street, in a third floor walk-up over a cut-rate music dealer. He had equipment to make microscopic photographs that can lay bare the inner details of translucent stones. Every diamond, including "perfect" diamonds, has so-called defects: flaws invisible under an ordinary glass. These form a pattern of structure along with the crystallography and give an accurate means of identifying stones. The method is rarely used, because it is too much bother, but my need wasn't ordinary.

The gemologist was a nice fellow, badly underweight. I had already arranged for him to do my work even though it was Sunday. It didn't take long. He took several shots of each stone and labeled them with exact weights. I gave him twenty dollars, put it on what I hoped was Moselle's expense account, and took off. He would mail me the developed photos; that could wait.

So I went downstairs, walked to Fifty-ninth Street and Sixth Avenue, and stared at Central Park for ten minutes. I didn't have a thing to do or a place to go. I went down Sixth Avenue until I stood between Moselle's Exchange and my hotel. It was all the home I had.

Forty-seventh Street was very quiet. I didn't see a soul on the block. I tried to figure how I could kill the day. I thought about blondes: natural like Helene Bender; with black roots like Rose.

None of them were waiting for me. I went slowly along the south side past the shutdown stores, wondering where all those people go on Sunday. Especially where could I go?

Across the street a man came out of a shabby doorway. He was really dressed for Sunday: gloves, a gray Homburg, and a topcoat over his arm. He was about seventy-five feet from me but my eyes are good, and he looked to me like the man I had passed on Friday. It was Stony Schultz's address – he had to be a foreigner; who else would have business in that building on Sunday?

The day was still on my hands; so I kept moving east. The man did the same. At Madison Avenue he turned north, so I did too. We passed St. Patrick's. He walked faster than I; as we approached Bartolomi's, he was half a

103

block ahead. I heard the shriek of an ambulance; I turned to watch it. It shot past; when I reached the corner, I noticed that the foreigner had vanished. He must have entered one of the office buildings.

I killed the day, killed a poor dinner, killed the evening, and went to bed. I dreamt, but nobody killed me. Monday morning came with not much to recommend it; I put on a different gray suit, a special from Bond's, two-pants, $69.50, and the well-dressed diamond peddler started on his rounds.

XVII

I first went into Corbin's, picked up Blok's diamonds, helped the boys lay out the merchandise as a good-will gesture, and shot out the door when a master of tedium named Bernardo came in. The morning was cool. I got peppy, something was going to break.

I began with Capple's Exchange. I had asked them to get me that emerald-cut, and I might as well go through with it. This time the famous painter himself was there. By the way Capple came over after the salesman greeted me, I knew he had heard something. The salesman had two stones for me to look at, neither quite what I wanted in price, weight, or quality, but he seemed willing to do business. He said they would try to get something closer to my needs by tomorrow. So for practice I turned to the master of the blue-white paintbrush and said:

"Want to look at a good buy, Mr. Capple?"

"A fast glance." The jelly-faced old gonef would look at anything. He was one of those men whose gray hair inspires contempt and their ill-health loathing. I displayed Moselle's four diamonds and watched him closely as he surveyed them.

"Nice merchandise," he remarked and picked up one of the doubtful items. "How much?"

I didn't want him to take that stone because I didn't really suspect him, so I said $1,760 per carat. He put it down without the slightest show of interest and certainly without recognition.

I went on, "The round one is a good buy at $1,265."

He studied it, gave me a look, and said," I don't need that goods now." He meant what he said, but he must have thought the diamond was hot, because he added, "I'd take it for stock at $1,200." If I had said yes it would have identified me as a peddler of stolen goods. I wanted that, but not at that price, so I smiled and shook my head.

He said, "I see you already have a good emerald-cut."

"Yes, but I want to show my customer more than one. Anyhow this is a little too good for him."

He put a loupe on it. "How much?"

"Fourteen-sixty."

At that price he could have it. The trouble was the old crook was in a position to buy as cheap as Barney Moselle.

He glanced at the paper for the weight. "You're not cheap enough for me, young fellow. A small operator might buy from you. I'd go $1,300 for it."

This was an offer to act as a fence. We jawed a little longer and I left, saying that I would be back Wednesday to see what they had. I was satisfied; word would be all over the street that my bargains were too good. Capple was a thief, but he wasn't in on my queer goods as far as I could tell, and he didn't have anything to fear. It was characteristic that he probably would give me merchandise on consignment. Since I had turned out to be a big-scale crook, I was a man to know – as an honest employee of Corbin's I was just another schmuck. I sighed for the cleanness of the old Chicago lineup and headed for Schultz's. Everybody spoke to me as they went by; I was getting to be somebody.

Schultz's stairway smelled no sweeter, nor did Schultz when he opened the door.

"Come in." Even he was more cordial.

"You wanted an emerald-cut?"

"Wanted? Who said I wanted?"

"You don't have a customer for a four-carat emerald-cut?"

"I might have a looker. An asker."

I opened Moselle's paper and let him see the stone Capple had offered $1,300 for. Moselle's cost was $1,420 per carat.

"Not a bad stone."

"Not bad."

106

"How much?"

"Thirteen-fifty." It was almost Capple's price for stolen goods; for Schultz it was a chance to make a quick, sure profit. Moselle would lose $300 if Schultz took me up on it.

He looked at me with complete understanding. "Thirteen hundred."

I folded the paper.

"It's not as if I needed it," he explained. So he didn't really have a buyer.

I opened the paper that held the hot diamond. "Here's one you won't pass up if you use diamonds."

He let it lie on his desk. "And?"

"Fourteen hundred per carat." Moselle had estimated it to be worth $1,620 – as it came from customs. The way Schultz picked it up, I saw he really did know the diamond market. I watched his mouth closely; I couldn't see his eyes after he bent over the stone.

"What's the weight?"

"Four-sixty-five."

He was looking harder and harder and I thought his hand shook. His mouth was such a disgusting affair at any time that I couldn't read a thing. Finally he laid it down.

"I don't need it."

My pulse went faster. "You should be able to make a quick turnover at that price."

"Not right now."

"Take it on memo for a few days." I was trying like hell to lose a thousand dollars.

"I don't have a prospect. If you haven't sold it in a week, give me a ring."

He wanted to get away from it; nothing else made sense. I presumed he didn't have $7,000 on hand, but he could have sold that diamond back to Moselle at $1,500 per carat if he wasn't afraid of it. Besides, I thought he looked even worse than usual. Something had scared him and it wasn't the idea of stolen goods. It was more like the smell of that diamond.

I left, went into the Wentworth bar and phoned Moselle. I was almost across the street from him, but I wasn't ready to walk in there yet. I gave Mr. Richards' name and got Barney quick enough.

"Yes, Mr. Richards."

"Barney, check your records to see if you gave Schultz a diamond that could have been switched for the one I'm carrying."

"It'll take time and then I won't be sure."

"It's worth it. I'll phone you later — maybe at your home."

"Right, Mr. Richards."

It was too early to eat, so I went back into the street and made three fast stops. All that I accomplished was to take three names off Moselle's list and to convince three more dealers that I was a crook. Then I crossed Sixth Avenue and went into the White Lily.

I was more tired than if I had put in the morning at Corbin's — evidently no longer accustomed to pavements. I slumped into a booth, loosened my shoes, and waited for Rose. She eventually swam into view; I took my corned beef on rye, cole slaw and a stein of beer, without encouraging talk. After I had eaten half of it, I tapped her hip as she floated by.

"Take a minute off when you get a chance. I have something for you."

She went white. I felt I might have too. How do I get into these things? Rose dropped down opposite me; table service stopped in the joint, as she set her large gray eyes on my face. I took a swallow of beer and said:

"I talked to Bud." She gasped. "He is an artist. He is known as Raphael D'Arle. I don't know which name, if either, is his right one. He's a successful man."

"Is he married?"

"Not as far as I know."

"Where is he?"

"Now just a minute, Rose. You've got to think. You've got to think what you're going to do before you do something foolish."

"*Where is he?*"

"Across the street. *Stay down a minute*.. You can see the studio from this doorway. But, Rose, ask yourself: what are you going to do? Before you crash in on him think out carefully what good it can do you. That's what you want, Rose – to do yourself some good. Do you want to land him or do you want to drive him away forever?"

I was wasting my breath. She didn't even say, where is he? She simply kept her eyes on mine. I saw beads of sweat on her forehead. Her hair was limp, her mouth unsteady, but her body was wound up tight enough to break her mainspring. I tried a little harder.

"He is a prominent painter doing a large business with a wealthy clientele. Fashionable women make a fuss over him. He will never marry you, Rose; not in a million years. I doubt if he'll even give you a bang. Moreover, he's a hard-boiled character, as you would have seen yourself if you weren't such a schmuck. You won't reach him with tears or hysterics. Nor can you frighten him. Let it go, Rose, he doesn't want any part of you. Whatever he wanted, he got it-"

"*He never got it!*"

"Then he's given it up. Be your age. It's finished. Done. Forget it."

We sat and stared at each other without a word until I wrote out the address. She read it carefully and put it inside her dress. I laid down the exact change, added her quarter, and left – I suppose she picked it up.

Fall certainly was early this year. It was so cold that I went back to the hotel and got my topcoat. Then I walked slowly along the street, thinking about my list of names. I passed Simminger's Pawn Shop; he was on the list, but those guys are very leery of stolen property. They are frequently victimized themselves, and they must work with the police. I would trust them further, that way, than almost anybody – their appraisals, of course, are generally slanted.

By this time I had reached Fifth Avenue. It was three o'clock; I couldn't do much more. Bartolomi was only a short distance away; I had always wanted to see what that kind of operation was like. I crossed over and headed for Madison Avenue. Why not? My topcoat was Bond Executive and I always wear a stetson.

It's one thing to admire Bartolomi's windows, this time displaying an exquisite assortment of earrings in diamonds, emeralds, and semiprecious stones; it's another thing entirely to find the entrance and get inside. It's one of those places where the door is small, discreet, solid brass, and kept closed. It will open if you work at it, after which you find yourself in an enclosed windowless vestibule. Then, mysteriously, an elderly gentlemen opens the inner door and you are free to spend your money; if you can find the artfully hidden merchandise. All this is done not so much to keep the jewelry in as to keep common people out.

I was free to spend my money, if I had any, but I couldn't imagine what on. I was in a room, perhaps thirty by thirty, furnished in a sickly Louis Fifteenth, and with *no* merchandise. The goods were contained, presumably, in hidden vaults to the rear.

A creaking salesman waited at my elbow. A slightly newer curiosity stood near the rear door. I presumed that several soldiers with fixed bayonets held the passage behind. I took a deep breath and conveyed to old skin-and-bones that I would like to see Mr. Bartolomi, and, what was more, for the base purpose of showing him goods.

"Everything we handle is imported, sir."

"My diamonds are imported."

He smiled faintly. "I imagine so. Mr. Bartolomi seldom examines merchandise except in the morning."

"I wouldn't bother him if I didn't think I had the right stuff. Please tell him that this merchandise must be disposed of at once and that I am not likely to get as good an opportunity to interest him as I have today."

"What is the name, please?"

"Handy. Saul Handy."

I thought he blinked. He spoke into a subdued phone; softly stressing my name, and then said, "This way please."

The second artifact moved up to replace him as he led me to the rear. I didn't know why I was following him. I had put myself so far out that I couldn't possibly accomplish anything after I did reach the lama. I would have to quote him ridiculous prices. Then either he would buy the goods for a beautiful loss to Moselle or else he would throw me out before I could say "blue white and perfect."

We rode a cute little elevator, decorated like the telephone in gold and ivory, up to the second floor, whence I was ushered into a combination office and workroom, with a fine walnut desk, two easy chairs, several large Old Master type paintings in big gilt frames, and two long tables covered with trays of assorted merchandise. Pins, earrings, rings, necklaces sparkled happily out of their delicately wrought gold and platinum. After I got my eyes off the goods, I looked at the gentleman attached to all this: a tall slender, distinctive personality, in a quiet, costly, custom gray suit. Dainty cuffs showed dainty cuff links, a single tietack punched a cruel hole through a handmade tie. The man put cool, gray disinterested eyes on me from behind the desk; a closer glance said that he was trying to decide if he had seen me before.

I didn't need to decide; he was the foreigner who had gone into and come out of Schultz's dump.

I had only one move. Before he could say a word, I said, "I have a diamond for you to look at, Mr. Bartolomi," and I laid the substituted diamond on his desk. He hadn't had time to ask me to sit down.

Bartolomi motioned toward a chair and looked indifferently at the stone. "I don't use much stuff in this size. None in the store; only a little for special customers or an occasional transaction in the trade."

This made sense since most of his business was in pieces. He could use a hundred half-carats easier than one big stone.

"How much?" he asked in a courteous, accentless voice. My heart sank as I said, "Thirteen-fifty per carat."

He glanced at me and took out his tweezers and glass. He peered at the diamond under an intense white light, and after a minute or so he settled down for a thorough study. Finally he said:

"Weight?"

"Four-sixty-five."

"Exact."

"Yes, sir." The question seemed unnecessary.

He held it a long time under his loupe before he set his tweezers down.

"Who are you, Mr. Handy? I don't know you." His face was inscrutable.

"I represent Herman Blok." I handed him one of Herman's cards. I felt very uncomfortable; if he checked with Blok, I would have some explaining to do all around. If he bought the diamond, what could I say to Moselle?

He said, "I have never done business with Blok."

I said, "I would like to get you started with us."

He said, "Does he import directly?"

I said, "Part of his goods is bought direct."

He said, "He must have good connections."

I said, "He has."

He said, "Does this stone come from Blok?"

It was not quite the right question. Why doubt it? His face was as blank as a slab of black onyx, and his relaxation was perfect – a well-established businessman, sitting in his own office, showing courtesy to a strange salesman before showing him the door. Still I decided to go in deeper. I said:

"That particular diamond is not one of Blok's."

"Whose is it?"

"Mine."

He nodded thoughtfully. "It's a good buy, but I don't need it." He could have made $600 without getting off his chair, at that price, and we both knew it.

I said, "I would like to leave it on consignment for a few days, Mr. Bartolomi, if you think you could turn it over."

I might as well have told him it was hot. He looked so appraisingly at me I expected him to put my head under the lamp.

"Are you the Mr. Handy I've read about?"

"I'm afraid so. You won't read any more about me."

"Odd experience you've had. Life can be very complex."

That one needed no reply, so I waited. He waited and then said, "I would like to hold the stone for one day – say until this time tomorrow."

"Thank you," said the master of losing propositions and I took out one of Blok's memo pads. I wrote him a memo as coolly as Henry could have done and offered him my fountain pen. He had his own imported eighteen-carat pen out; he signed, first and last name. I gave him his copy. We got up.

"I might have something else you could use by tomorrow," I remarked.

"By all means, Mr. Handy."

He actually walked me to the elevator. He was the politest guy that ever went into Stony Schultz's office. In the corner of the room a closet door stood slightly ajar and I thought I glimpsed a Homburg hat. I was really in the class this time – up to my ears. The question was, outside of risking a loss of over a thousand dollars, what had I accomplished?

I didn't know, so I zoomed out of the elevator and glided cautiously past the two mummies. Needless to say, no one was trying to buy anything. At the door I turned, I still don't know why, and said to the attenuated servitor:

"Do you wait on Mrs. Edward Bender personally?"

"Mrs. Bender of Crestmere? I have, at times. Usually, of course, Mr. Bartolomi takes care of her."

"Of course," I murmured. "Lovely person, isn't she?"

"Oh, indeed. Lovely."

I went through the delousing chamber and headed for a phone booth. Moselle spoke almost as soon as I mentioned Mr. Richards.

"Well, Barney?"

"That wasn't a bad guess you made, Mr. Richards. The answer is affirmative."

"S.S. had it?"

"Yes."

"About when?"

"About July 16, this year."

"How long out?"

"Can't be sure. Not too long."

"How can you be certain of the date?"

"Henry remembers. It was his last transaction before going on vacation. It kept him from leaving early."

"Did he have the other one?"

"That I can't tell. I doubt it. We don't do much business with him."

We hung up. I was sure I had something; what, was anybody's guess.

Then I remembered I had used Blok's memo form for Moselle's diamond. If Bartolomi should grasp the meaning of that, and decide to take advantage, how the hell would I get the goods back? The stone wasn't Blok's and I couldn't possibly show it was mine. Some diamond trader!

XVIII

I couldn't waste much time over $7,000 diamonds, because I knew I had opened something. Something was vibrating around me; something was in the air. It came from near me – not too near. It came from where I was looking. I took a fix on that spot and I went where the fix pointed.

It pointed at Stony Schultz. I went diagonally across the street like a sleepwalker and up those stairs again. I had hardly left the place, but that didn't bother me. The way the vibrations were steering I could have been a missile.

The high little wooden vestibule was still where I had left it. Schultz's head came through the peephole the same way as before. The alarm for the Holmes ran up the side of the door in the same place. The two setters were still bent over their table.

But something had changed. Something had been added. Stony had company. Lila Moselle was there.

Schultz was changed, too. He wasn't himself at all; the ferment had gone out of that piece of dough and what lay in the pan was soggy. Stony was scared; I could smell fear like sewer gas. But I wasn't doing much sniffing because I was all eyes and my eyes were all for Lila.

"Slumming, Mrs. Moselle?" Clichés ooze out of me when I'm confused.

She gleamed as she always gleamed, beautiful, continental, sleek, efficient, friendly, and remote. She was very remote. I could feel her rushing closer, but it was a closing in from a far place, like a ski jumper's coming in off Mt. Shasta.

"I often buy my stones from Mr. Schultz," she said cordially. "He often has exactly what I need."

115

We were shaking hands through wind-swept spaces. My confusion hadn't diminished.

"*You* need stones from *him?*"

Her smile was all warmth, understanding, friendship. "Not *diamonds*, Mr. Handy. Not diamonds. Semiprecious stones. Mr. Schultz was to have had some very fine turquoise for me today."

"They didn't come in," said Schultz. "Tomorrow, I think."

She could have spared herself a climb up some dirty stairs by picking up the phone, but what I said was:

"I didn't realize you carried your designing to the point of selecting the stones yourself."

Actually what I thought didn't count a quarter point, because I didn't know enough about really fine pieces to have an opinion. Ordinarily the designer merely draws the design. A modelmaker makes the piece, the proprietor selects the goods to set it in, a setter does the setting, and so on.

"How could I make them without the stones?" Her surprise was genuine; we were almost in the same world now.

I took this in. "You make your own jewelry?"

"Of course."

"With your own hands?"

She held out small, sophisticated fingers:

"With these little piggies."

"Settings too?"

"Settings too."

I was impresseed. "I didn't know anybody could do top work in designing, jewelry making, and in setting."

"Amateurs can. Some amateurs."

"You're not an amateur."

"I am really. I do it for love."

The word "love" slurred. She was close, the black eyes shining on mine, her breath faintly audible. But Schultz!

I said, "You must have one of those ducky little amateur studios somewhere."

"Would you like to see it?"

"I would love," I said gallantly, "to see where you do your etchings."

"I'll show you now," she said, "if you can finish your business with Mr. Schultz."

I turned to the devaluated satyr. "You know, Stony, you made a mistake passing up my goods today. Guess who has taken the big one."

"You found a schnook?" He was interested.

"Battista Bartolomi."

He didn't change much – he always looked like a piece of putty. Lila started slightly, as she naturally would.

"If you can supply Battista," she said, "you will have a very good account."

"Tops," said Schultz. "Tops."

"Tops," I said. "Do you want to see more of my goods?"

"Now? What?"

"Not now. I haven't anything with me you haven't seen. But I can have."

"Anytime. Anytime."

"I'll be back. Tomorrow maybe."

"Sure. Tomorrow. Sure."

I turned to Lila. "Are you going, Mrs. Moselle?"

"Since Mr. Schultz hasn't the turquoise. I hope you are working on it, Stony."

"Yes, I'm working on it. I'll have them tomorrow maybe. Tomorrow. A beautiful package." He brought his fingers to his lips, kissed them vigorously. "Beautiful. You know that stuff can be hard to get."

"Not for you, Stony. You can find them for me if you want to. Shall we go, Mr. Handy?"

We went. I delicately preceded her down the stairs and awaited her at the foot. She descended as imperturbably as Bartolomi had gone up. She looked as though she would have been a success with Bartolomi – they were such an engraved, buffed, enameled couple. Engine-turned maybe.

I couldn't help thinking that those crumby stairs had some classy climbers.

The lights of the show windows glowed brightly in the dusk.

"Do you really want to see my workshop, Mr. Handy?"

"I certainly do."

"You *are* interested in the arts."

"Deeply."

"My studio is in Barney's building."

It figured. We walked the few yards to the entrance, I none too comfortable about being seen alongside the wife of the man I was supposed to have quarreled with.

There are two entrances to Moselle's building: one through the exchange, the other from the street through a little vestibule. An elevator goes to the office building above. Fortunately she took this entrance.

We got off on the fourth floor and went to a door adjoining Moselle's clerical offices. She unlocked it; it had Holmes protection, which rang out as usual. She gave the answering signal, and removed two trip-cords strung along the floor.

The room was a neat little affair, completely equipped. It held a designing board, jeweler's bench, motor with the usual polishing and grinding accessories, oxygen torch for platinum, a separate bench with engraver's and setter's tools, a hotbox for quick drying, and a very modern miniature steamer for the indispensable cleaning. More unusual, she had a little furnace which could be used either as a kiln for enameling or as a smelter to reduce old metal.

Everything was as clean as a dentists office; except for that, it could have been one of a thousand rooms on the block shared by the usual jeweler, setter, engraver trio. But one touch revealed the amateur: a small bookcase filled with volumes whose large size suggested art books. And there was an easy chair with a reading lamp.

"The studio of the artist," she said, with a dancer's sweep of her most unworkmanlike hands. "Your third in three days. You have become one of the cognoscenti."

"My third," I agreed thoughtfully.

"Isn't that correct?"

I asked slowly, "You have seen Mr. D'Arle since Saturday?"

"Yes. I mentioned your interest. He mentioned your visit."

"My interest is rising. Did he seem flattered?"

"Interested certainly."

"Interesting" (and curious). "So this is where you make those famous Italian masterpieces."

"I do only modern things. Bartolomi's traditional patterns are imported. And I never worked for Battista here. But some stuff has come from this room since those days, which I rather liked. Hollywood, Houston, Miami, Chicago, have used pieces made here."

I glanced at the benches. "You don't seem to have anything under way. Is it in the vaults?"

"It would be but I don't do much now. Won't you sit down, Mr. Handy?"

I sank gratefully into the easy chair. "You must be the only person in the business, Mrs. Moselle, who calls me mister."

She smiled gaily. "Then it is Lila and Saul." She sat before her jeweler's bench, a yard from me.

I looked curiously about the room. Her speech was bothering me; it had a homey ring which contradicted the Monaco personality.

"Lila," I asked by way of practice on her name, "are you from Illinois?"

"Missouri."

I hadn't expected Missouri – that's almost Mason and Dixon.

"St. Louis perhaps?"

"No." She wasn't coming in for old home week. Not that she minded questions but that she preferred to ask them. She went on:

"So you're a detective."

"I am?"

"It's hardly a secret."

Was she asking or telling? "It's no secret that I was once a policeman."

"Once a sleuth – "

"Don't you believe it."

The little smelter caught my eye. "What do you need that for? You surely don't make castings."

"I don't make cast jewelry. That's a kiln. I'm also an

119

enameler. Besides, it's a convenience not to give out my scrap. Sometimes I change the alloy for special results."

"You work up everything out of the raw metal?"

"Just like a wood carver."

I noticed a ten-inch length of what looked like iron pipe lying on the bench. I reached for it; her hand was there first and she picked it up, rising to her feet as she did so. I sat looking up at her; her face was strange.

"How," I asked, "did that thing get on this bench?"

She stood for a moment, undecided for once, turned slightly, swung back to me and said:

"Here."

She held out the tube lightly. I took it in the same way and it fell through my relaxed fingers to the floor with a heavy thud.

"What the hell – "

She smiled apologetically. "A poor joke."

I picked up the dirty gray pipe reverently. It seemed to weigh a ton.

"Platinum?"

She nodded. Her eyes were bright and hot; I got my first intimation that I was going to know Lila Moselle better. I hefted the massive little thing. Platinum is four times heavier than iron; the tube was equivalent to an iron pipe of the same cross section three feet long.

"You carve rings from this?"

"Some kinds. Sometimes I work from a solid block. The tube saves time, of course."

She was an expert all right. She didn't look it. I examined her slender white wrists.

"It's a wonder you have the strength to hand this to me the way you did."

The eyes, again like the fading spot on a television screen, went into mine.

"I'm a tennis player. And a horsewoman."

And a good one, I'd have bet. I laid the platinum on the bench using both hands to avoid needless banging. She asked quietly:

"Are you getting anywhere for Barney?"

"*With* Barney you mean? I think we may soon work out a settlement."

She was dead-pan against the hot eyes. I tried to look like a retail clerk out of work which should have been easy. To stop the questions, I said:

"Artist, workman, tennis player, woman of the great world – you seem to be able to do many things."

"Many things. Especially woman of the world," and in one curving motion she was down deep into my lap, one hand behind my head, one on my cheek, and her lips molding mine.

I couldn't move or talk. Her hard athlete's body slithered in its silk, her hand clamped my head. I touched her gingerly, mostly from surprise. But that did it. I felt a rushing like a hurricane, my body became a throbbing, swelling hollow tube, I heard myself give a deep moan, and I had half her clothes off when the eye of the storm must have passed over me.

"Lila – Barney – I can't – "

Not a word came out of her. One hand ripped at my shirt while the other grew to my head. I hadn't touched a woman in weeks; it would have been over in a minute, but that big murderous Israeli diamond danced before my eyes, and I could see Moselle ready to cover me to do the right thing.

"Lila, I can't. Not Barney."

I'm an athlete too. I put my last ounce of strength into those faltering legs and managed to stand up without throwing her to the floor. We stood breast to breast, I bowed over her. Her hand hadn't moved.

"I want to, Lila. I want to."

The pressure on my neck became unendurable. We would both have fallen but as suddenly as they had seized me her arms dropped.

My arms dropped. I pulled in a gasp of air. She scarcely seemed to breath at all, but she was dead-white and her eyes were needles.

"Lila, I'm sorry. I'll be sorry all my life. I can't – I'm getting out of here. Before – I can't."

I strode across the room, grabbed my coat and hat,

121

pulled the door open and went through it, she standing like a raped danseuse in the middle of the floor, as erect as an obelisk and as rigid. God knows what she thought. I know what I felt.

XIX

It was dark when my burning flesh felt the air outside. I was shaking, dizzy, and sweating furiously. I leaned against Moselle's building and waited for the blood to settle.

The street was quiet now. Windows were pulled, only Fogelman was still putting the goods away. The lights were going out. A few people headed for the subways and buses. The Wentworth bar looked warm and busy. Corbin's was dark; my bosses had gone to their suburbs.

I could see the White Lily; Rose would have left at five o'clock.

I started down Sixth Avenue toward Forty-second Street. A small world rode with me; vibrant, sensual, expensive; the odors, the heartbeat, the overpowering hands of Lila. I felt let down. I had missed something which wouldn't come again – not to me. What she had wanted from me I didn't know; what I had lost was the Golden Fleece. Some men don't get some things.

I noticed a woman crossing the sidewalk: bigger than Lila, slightly overdressed, at least for her, and too tightly dressed. She entered a building almost in front of me. I passed on and then looked back. It was Raphael D'Arle's address; the stocky one was Rose. I wished her luck and kept going. She wouldn't find any.

I couldn't eat and I didn't want to drink. I went into one of the fleabags on Forty-second Street and sat through two stupid pictures waiting for Lila to fade away. I came out under a blinding canopy of light, walked back to my hotel, stopped in the hotel coffee shop for a sandwich which no hunger could flavour, and went through the rear door into the drab lobby which is the entrance to my home.

Cassidy and his ghost were talking to the desk clerk. They didn't see me. I stood and studied the uninviting trio. Then I came up behind them and asked:

"Waiting for someone?"

They turned as if I had said, "Stick 'em up!"

"Did you," I went on, "forget something?"

No answer.

"You're now on the vice squad?"

Silence.

"Pickpocket detail, perhaps?"

They were two Indians.

"Is there anything *I* can do for you?"

The act changed. Cassidy said:

"This way." He jerked his thumb toward the street door.

The night man at the desk was almost a nice fellow compared to the day crumb. Two old and shabby residents made the rest of the harsh-lit audience.

"Where to?" I asked.

"We'll lead the way."

It was no place to make a scene. I moved along the line of the pointed thumb.

Outside we walked west. We turned at Sixth Avenue, which looked worse than usual, and we started down the street. I was wondering; no cop walks if he can ride; they're like cowboys.

"Car break down?"

"We won't need it yet."

We passed Forty-seventh Street and crossed the Avenue of the Dirty Americas. Another block and I saw policemen and police cars. They were gathered about one entrance, as they would be. I felt right at home when we got up to them – Raphael D'Arle's home.

There were three squad cars, an ambulance, two uniformed policemen and a plain-clothes man I recognized from homicide. Cassidy led the way upstairs, I following. The shadow came up behind me. D'Arle's studio was lit as if for a new showing, and was cluttered with photographers, lab men, and newspapermen.

All the ingredients were there for a successful show: glaring paintings, glaring faces, overpowering color, and spectral eyes. My senses must have been at fever pitch because I could see everybody and everything at once: the postured people, the phony art, the bar (but nobody serving!), the bookcase, the easel on the floor, the Maori spear, the Samoan canoe paddle, the Chinese bronzes, the African sculpture – the whole flotsam of an artist's showroom, all brought into one focus – a masterpiece of concrete expressionism. But the central object, the big foreground subject, wasn't in sight. I didn't see Raphael.

Then I saw her. Rose, on a painter's stool, looked toward me, her eyes like big grapes, the rest of the face dissolved into something spongy, the whole woman a coagulated bulk of stupified grief or fear.

I went up to her; my escort stayed near me.

"What's wrong, Rose?"

She didn't answer. I don't know if she knew me or not. I did see that she looked sloppy although she was wearing the same dress she had on four hours earlier. She was dirty, as if she had been splashed by mud. But the mud was reddish – reddish brown – on her arms, bosom, hair, and skirt. I turned to Cassidy.

"What's happened?"

"You don't know?"

"Cut it, Cassidy. What happened to her?"

"You know her?"

"Yes, I know her. *Are you hurt, Rose?*"

She got up suddenly and fell on me, her big hairdo pushing into my face, her bloody arms around my neck. A slight smell of sweat suggested that she had dressed after work without stopping to bathe. And she was sobbing.

I patted her back a few times and lifted her head so I could see her face.

"Rose – "

"He's dead."

I had known it, known it as soon as I saw the squad cars. I looked over her head at Cassidy.

"With a blunt instrument?"

His face was rock.

"Where is he?"

Cassidy swung his head toward the windows. There was

an easy chair, filled up, and a sheet over it. I put Rose back on the stool.

"May I see him?"

We walked to the bundle and Cassidy uncovered some of it. It could have been worse, apparently one blow, but it's never a pleasure.

Cassidy said, "Can you confirm the identification?"

"It's the painter, Raphael D'Arle."

"Friend of yours?"

"Only met him once."

"When?"

"Saturday."

"Here?"

"Yes."

We both waited for the other.

I said, "Do you know who did it?"

He motioned toward Rose. "It's between you two."

"It wasn't her."

"Is that a confession?"

I stared at his huge body with its big round head and bleak eyes. "Let's pretend we're policemen," I said. "It is not a confession; it is a statement. She's no killer."

"Somebody is. And with a blunt instrument."

It seemed funny to me, too. Two murders, each tied to me, more or less, and both done the same way.

"I would like," I said carefully, "to know more about this."

"You will. Downtown."

We went. Downtown, in two different cars, through the streets of New York, sirens blowing some of the time, out of the feverish traffic of Times Square into the absolute silence of City Hall at night. Through corridors into cubicles, Rose and me kept separate. I seemed to be in a room I had known before; no wonder – there sat Marder and Druckman. We sat around a little table like a board of directors.

Cassidy opened it. "Do you have that photograph of the deceased with you?"

I had. I had put it in my wallet intending to give it back to Rose, and I was sitting on it.

"How did you know I had it?" I asked as I tossed it over.

"I remembered your last visit."

I had had it among my effects. But that Cassidy should have remembered the face was remarkable; it was my first intimation that he really might be a detective.

"How could you remember a thing like that, sergeant?"

The respect in my voice didn't displease him, "I kind of thought I knew the guy."

"Had D'Arle a record?"

"We're checking. Who gave you this picture?"

Now I was on the spot. I couldn't know what ideas they had about Rose and me. I said cautiously:

"Ask me that question a little later, sergeant. Let me answer some of your other questions."

"Don't you like that question? Want time to figure a different story?"

"What story?"

He came around the table and pushed his face into mine. The head was like a medicine ball, gigantic; he must have needed a seven and three-quarters hat. At that range it looked as big as the face of a totem pole. He roared against my eyes:

"The story you're going to tell where you were between nine and eleven tonight."

"In the movies."

"*What* movie?"

"A lousy one."

"You're a lousy liar. What theater?"

"The Bijou."

He showed his disgust. Since the pictures were old, I could have seen them years ago.

"Anybody see you in the theater?"

"Only Cary Grant."

"Bright boy, you don't have an alibi. You don't have an alibi at all. As one old-time detective to another, I advise you to come clean. If you don't give us the truth and all of it, I'm booking you for accessory to murder."

He had told me something. "Who's my principal?"

"The bloody lady who saw him last."

"You think I use women to kill my victims?"

"I think you set him up for her."

In a sense I had, if she had done it. I would have given something for ten minutes' conversation with Rose. I still don't know how I might have played it though because something Cassidy had said suddenly began to tap a Morse code in my skull.

"One minute, sergeant. Could I look at that photo?"

He was so surprised that he gave it to me. I studied the plumpish, rather unhappy face and tried to resurrect the man I had seen last Saturday. And as I tried the Morse code got louder and louder.

"Sergeant," I asked, "did you mean that this photo suggested someone you knew?"

"What else?"

"Lieutenant, have you checked Light out for aliases and city of origin?"

"We have. He seems to be the same man as Alberto Carlo, no previous convictions, wanted for bank robbery in Boise, Idaho."

I kept looking at that photo. "And his birthplace?"

"Muskingdon, Idaho."

I turned to Cassidy. "You don't know it, sergeant, but your cop's memory for faces has half solved two cases, I think." I tapped the picture. "Check this one out for aliases and place of birth. And check him in Muskingdon."

Cassidy reached for the photo and the four policemen huddled over it. I took in the group for a minute and asked:

"What have you got on Rose?"

Cassidy answered, "She walked into an officer in the street, in front of the scene of the murder, dripping the victim's blood."

"What's her story?"

"She found him that way."

"Going to hold her?"

"I need my job — you too."

"Me what?"

"Hold you."

"Why Rose? Why doubt her story?"

"What do you think we are, for Christ's sake? You and

128

she were in on something connected with this D'Arle. Either blackmail or robbery; we'll find that later. You are also a guy who turns up battered corpses. She said you gave her D'Arle's address. Claims she didn't know it until this morning. You have his picture. She must have given it to you; he may be related to the other victim. Don't you think we should at least hold the two of you for questioning? What do they do in Chicago? Even if you had an alibi, I'd hold you. All we don't know is which one of you swung the weapon and why. And we'll find that."

"You can't," I said calmly. "There is no motive and neither of us killed him, so we can't be tied in. Holding me would be stupid. You might put Rose in the hospital for one night to make sure she doesn't hurt herself. She's in shock."

"Our next commissioner," Druckman remarked.

"Could I talk to Rose?" I asked.

Cassidy turned to his partner. "Bring her in."

We waited two or three minutes. What a dreary scene it was! The cement cubicle, the stark chairs and table, the brutal light; Marder, lean, ugly, eagle-beaked; Druckman, big, blockish, blunt-featured; Cassidy, huge, round, snub-nosed. I couldn't help wondering whether I looked so revolting, so inhuman.

Then Rose came in. I looked into her stupified eyes. "Rose, tell me what happened."

She blinked at me.

"Did you see him earlier in the day?"

She came to, a little. "Oh, yes."

"When?"

"Today."

"*When?* Right after I saw you?"

"Yes."

"Was it two, three o'clock?"

"Maybe."

"What did you do – cross the street in your uniform?"

"Yes."

"He was in good shape?"

"Oh, yes."

"How did it go?"

"He got rid of me."

"Rose, I saw you going into his place around seven o'clock. You were dressed. Did you change on the job?"

"I went home and changed."

"Did you see him then?"

"No. Nobody answered."

"What did you do?"

"Sat in a bar and tried again."

"How many times?"

"Three times."

"When was the last time?"

She shuddered violently – shuddered and shook and trembled.

"She needs a doctor," I said to Cassidy. "Rose, was it around ten, eleven o'clock?"

"I guess so."

"Did you knock on the door?"

"No."

"Why not?"

"It was open."

"Were the lights on?"

"I don't know. I think so."

"Did you walk in?"

"Yes."

"Who was there?"

She passed out. I turned to Cassidy as Marder got up to call a matron. "You'll have to hospitalize her. When she comes to, she'll tell you that she looked around the studio, maybe called his name, found him in the chair or on the floor, tried to help him, realized the stuff was blood, and ran screaming out of the house. And that's all you'll ever get out of her because that's all there will be to get."

We sat quiet until two matrons came. Partner helped them get her out of the room. Then the five of us looked at each other. There wasn't much else to do; not one of us knew the next move. Certainly I didn't, except that I wanted out of there.

Finally Cassidy said, "Would you mind telling us now where you got that painter's photograph?"

"From Rose."

"Why?"

"She asked me to find him."

"For how much?"

"You know better than that, sergeant."

"Why did she want to find him?"

"She was in love with him."

Marder cut in. "That certainly gives a motive."

"Not in itself, lieutenant. Love and murder aren't like love and marriage. They don't necessarily go together."

"No," Cassidy said, "but here they are together. How come the dame asked *you* to find him?"

"She knew me from the restaurant. She's been serving me for years. If you call it service."

"She must have known you were a guy who might find somebody."

"I had told her that I used to be a cop."

Druckman decided to come in, "Stirring up a little unlicensed business?"

I didn't answer. Marder took it up.

"I would like an account of your movements – all of them – between the time you saw Bender and eleven o'clock tonight."

I told them. I told them every little thing I had done. Only no reasons. I told them I had seen Moselle about the diamond, but not that he had hired me to look into the matter. I told them about Blok, Schultz, Capple and Bartolomi, but I didn't mention that the goods I had offered was baited. I told them that I got D'Arle's address from Quinones. I saw no need to mention Lila, because, after all, she had used less than an hour of my time.

Marder was very dissatisfied. "It's a lot of nothing. What are you up to, Handy?"

"Up to? I don't understand, lieutenant."

"What's all the running around for?"

"I have to do something."

"Have you lost your job?"

"Not exactly."

"What does that mean?"

"I'm not fired, but my employers would just as soon I stayed away for a few days. – That's as of this morning.

131

When *this* gets out, I'll be lucky if I can get a job on the waterfront."

"You won't need one," Druckman decided. "Not where you're going."

"I think," Marder said, "you won't keep one long unless you stop whatever you're up to."

"What do you mean?"

"I think you'll be a case for homicide. And not as a suspect."

"Why?"

"Because you're up to your ears in police business and you're not set to take it. I think that if the sergeant would book you and keep you for a few weeks, it might be the one thing that would spare us another corpse. – That's besides anything crooked you're involved in."

I turned to Cassidy. "Does the lieutenant mean, sergeant, that you're going to release me?"

Cassidy got up. "Take over," he said to his dreary follower. "Get a detailed statement. Check it out."

"And him?"

"Do whatever you want with the goddam ghoul."

XX

City Hall Park is a miserable blot of cement and dirt, at three o'clock in the morning. I had been tempted to ask for a cell for the night, but I didn't (who ever did?), so there I stood, a free man in the black loneliness of that empty city, and looked on a moonless sky. It topped a spotting of foggy street lights, a few huddled cars, and one news truck plugging uptown, loaded, no doubt, with pictures of Rose's eyes, D'Arle's skull, Cassidy's pudding face, and maybe even a chance shot of a baffled, unemployed jewelry salesman.

I couldn't see a coffee shop open. I went down into the subway – *it* looked like a burial trench dug in a Scranton slag heap – went back to my cottage, avoided the face of the night man, endured the "late tonight" from the elevator operator, and fell into bed.

I slept for five hours and that was that. After a shower, I emerged into a rainy morning and had breakfast in Schraffts, so help me.

Now all I needed was a murderer or two and a few jewelry thieves.

I didn't worry about Rose and the police. They would have to release her as soon as they could get her out of the hospital. Nothing could implicate her except the murder weapon with her fingerprints on it, and, once again, they didn't have the murder weapon.

Which was strange, for two blunt instrument killings.

I bought a paper (I hadn't wanted one on an empty stomach) and found the murder played up complete with artistic evaluations of Raphael's contribution to New York abstract expressionism and a reproduction of one of his most admired works, now owned by Mrs. Edward Bender of Crestmere; and with an appalling photo of Rose looking as if she had been bludgeoned out of all humanity; but there wasn't a line about me. I bought the other tabloid and it was the same, except that they had a profile of Rose which didn't make her such a golem. No Saul Handy.

I turned this over a few times, knitted up some details such as (1) I hadn't been held, notwithstanding two corpses; (2) Marder had been very solicitous about my health; (3) Marder had needlessly intruded himself into two homicide investigations; and concluded (4) either they were giving me enough rope or else I was fish-bait on police hooks.

So I went to a phone booth and called Marder. He answered:

"Yes?"

"Two questions. One: Did you find anything in D'Arle's studio which connects up to the clues in my car?"

"What's your second question?"

"Did you find a link between D'Arle and Light?"

"Yes."

"For both?"

"Yes."

I took a long breath. "Thanks, lieutenant."

"Handy – "

"Yes?"

"Phone me tonight and tell me how you make out."

"Make out? How?"

"Staying alive, for one thing."

"I'll call you."

Such concern! Who was using whom?

Forty-seventh Street is not gay in a chill autumn rain. The lighted windows are bright, but the empty, windswept street grates on the buying mood. In every store, exchange, or booth overweight men and women look emptily about, missing their daylong pinpricks, their familiar irritations. They know nothing of relaxation and have forgotten peace; they are wound alarm clocks trying to ring – overtaxed boilers looking for safety valves, or maybe free running escapements with no balance wheels to control.

I went into Corbin's first. Even that circus was empty.

"Good morning, Saul," said Murray and Jake. "Anything new?"

"Another body," I said casually. "But don't tell anyone about me – not until it breaks in the papers."

"Whatever you say, Saul." They wouldn't tell anybody. That's a funny thing about people; those boys were so used to keeping their business to themselves that they would probably have kept the blowing up of Moscow confidential if you had asked them to.

Jake added, "Anybody we know?"

"No such luck. You never heard of him."

"One of your girl friends? I've kinda figured you for a sex fiend."

"With a club?"

"Jesus! Another of those?"

I spread my arms.

"When?"

"Last night."

"This guy around the corner?"

"That's the one."

"Such a fancy guy!"

"Eighteen karat."

By this time they had stopped whatever they were doing and were huddled with me. I watched the door against unwanted persons trying to buy things.

Jake said, "Isn't is dangerous hanging around murder?"

"I don't know," I answered honestly. Coincidence or fate; I couldn't tell.

"The dame isn't your waitress, is she?"

"She is."

"Saul," Murray said enviously, "I underrated you. When are you coming back to work?"

"Next week, I think." I breezed on. Such confidence I had! "It should be cleaned up by then."

Ada Mann was showing in the door. I said, "I'm off for now. I'll keep you posted." And I ran before Ada could latch onto me. – They were certainly a couple of guys with very steady nerves. As long as I didn't kill one of them, they figured it was none of their business what I did on the outside.

So I walked over to the address of a leading New York financier, took the elevator to the sixteenth floor, room 34, and asked the blonde to see Mr. Bender.

"Have you an appointment, Mr. Handy?"

"Just say it's Bloody Head Handy."

She confided briefly in the telephone.

Black-suit came out within a couple of minutes and considerately held the door for me. I led the way to the businessman's sanctum. Bender was in position, a phone at his ear, a phone lying on the desk, and a phone ringing beside it. I waited until he cleared the lines with some Chinese-like syllables. Then we inspected each other.

He said, "Is this visit necessary?"

"Is it?"

"What do you mean?"

"You don't know?"

"What?"

This could have gone on for years, so I said, "Do you know if Al Light had a brother?"

"Don't you?"

"I think I do."

"You probably think right."

"Would you know where I can find him?"

"Try the morgue."

So that was that. I said, "Do you know who would want to kill little brother?"

"No."

"Is there a connection between Light's killing and this one?"

"Yes."

"What?"

"You."

"Do you know anything that might bear on this murder at all?"

"Is that what the police want to know?"

"Wouldn't they?" I thought he was uncomfortable.

He said, "What did you come here for?"

"I want you to let me have that diamond you found in Light's apartment. For two days."

That got him. Even black-suit stirred.

"Why?"

"I want to show it to somebody."

"Who?"

"A suspect."

He took a breather. "Light's murderer?"

"A handful of hot merchandise. Maybe the murderer."

"What good will that do?"

"He may recognize it."

"Suppose the police find it on you?"

"It won't matter if it isn't hot. If it is, I'll say my suspect gave it to me."

"So I lose it."

"What good is it to you if it's hot?"

He looked at black-suit. "This guy is a character. Think you can find him if we need him?"

"I can find him."

Bender got up, went to the safe, took out an envelope and gave it to me. I pinched the stone inside.

"Want a memorandum?" I asked.

He laughed harshly. "I won't forget."

"See you Thursday." I turned to go.

"What about my money?"

"This week, I think."

"What's the stall?"

I thought he said it curiously, as if he really wondered why.

"I could get it for you today," I admitted, facing him, "but I want you to think about me this week."

"Not next week?"

I gave him a steady one. "Next week shouldn't be necessary."

He nodded. "Guess right this time. Especially when you show that diamond."

I left, the orderly supporting me through the corridor. When the door closed between us, I looked over the platinum goods in the reception room – her hairdo was higher than a shako.

"The way things are warming up," I said, "you can say The Mr. Handy on my next call."

"Not in Crestmere," she said, which showed that she hadn't bleached all the brains out. I exchanged a wink for a smile and left.

I hurried over to Herman Blok's. There was a lot to do but I couldn't hold his goods any longer without putting in an appearance. I hoped my name would stay out of the evening papers so I could be a diamond salesman for a few more days, but even so, Herman was entitled to a look at his stones. But he was out. I left word that I would be back that day.

Capple's Exchange was next. The salesman knew me now. He showed an emerald-cut, about three and one-half carats, not too fine for my purpose, and within three minutes I was in the street with the stone in my pocket. Funny world – my credit seemed to have gone up.

And now, Schultz. He was out but expected back any minute. I sat in the tiny partitioned anteroom. For five minutes I dreamed about Moselle, Henry, Marder, Light, Bender, D'Arle, Rose, Bartolomi, and how they fitted into the flavorless life of Saul Handy. They had brought me up a long way; two weeks ago I was nobody in the jewelry business and less any place else. Now I was an object of impassioned concern to the whole police department and every gonef on the street was trying to do business with me.

What would become of Rose?

A choice specimen of the trade came through the door.

"Hello, Stony."

"How's the boy, Saul?"

We sat, presently, at his chewed-up desk. I opened Capple's paper and let him inspect the goods.

"Not too good."

"That's right."

"This supposed to be white?"

"So they tell me."

"Not even silver cape. Looks like something came out of your kidney."

"Should I argue with you, Stony?"

"How much?"

"Eight-twenty per carat." It was my cost.

He folded the paper without a word and handed it to me, which was what I had expected. He never would pay Manny Capple's memo price unless he needed goods bad. I handed him another paper: Bender's diamond.

He watched it flicker on the desk with no interest at all, picked it up, put his loupe on it, made a face as he took in the dead look, settled down to a careful examination, and laid it down.

"Not for me."

He hadn't asked the price. I looked him in the eye and said, "Not for $3,000?"

No matter how you valued the stone, he could have turned a profit at that price. If he had taken me up on it, I would have said I was kidding.

But he didn't. Instead, he said, "Saul, I wonder if you and I couldn't do business the other way around?"

"How do you mean?"

"Couldn't you sell a few things for me?"

"Dyed turquoise?"

He said quietly, "I have a few diamonds."

I didn't ask him why he needed me. "Tell me some more."

He went to his safe, came back with four papers, and opened them. There were two rounds, an emerald-cut and a marquise – a fortune in diamonds. The smallest was the emerald-cut, about four carats. I had never seen a finer stone. It had a minor flaw at one corner which would have been hidden when set. I had the feeling that if the stone I had shown him from Capple had been the right match in size and of a better color, I would have got it back in about three days, with a small flaw in the corner. Who would have made an issue of that? A fair exchange is no robbery – not when the goods comes back better than it went out. Manny Capple would have made such swaps all day long. – Even with a sparkle of murder? Maybe.

"You want me to peddle this?"

"Can you?"

"How much?"

139

He wrote out a price list on a scrap of paper. "This is what I get."

The prices were about 25 per cent below wholesale, which was a damn good price for a fence, but he wouldn't have needed me for less than that because then he could have recut them. I could have sold them in one day and made 10 per cent for myself, if –

"Whose do I say they are?"

"You're a broker. Must you say?"

It was true. I didn't need to unless the police did the asking, but that was quite an if. He might have been testing me for thieves' honor, so I said:

"Let me try these two." I pointed to the emerald-cut and the marquise. They would be the easiest to identify.

"Glad to, Saul, glad to." Already he was doing me a favor.

"How often do you want a report?"

"I think I should hear from you in a day or two."

It was as much trust as I had earned. We would both be on rotten limbs when I walked out with the stones. I would have very hot merchandise on me and no way in the world to explain where I got it. If I named Schultz, he would simply deny it. Gummed up as I already was, who would believe me? On the other hand, he ran the risk that I would never come back with goods or money. How could he prosecute? Suppose I asked where he got them? – Of course, he might be relying on underworld connections which could recover anything. He seemed to have got over yesterday's fear.

I said, "Write them up. Exact weights, please."

He said, "I don't care about weights."

I said, "I do."

He said, "Why so technical?"

I said, "My customers like to know such things."

He hesitated. Weights would mean that we each had something on the other. No weights meant nothing in writing. The stones would have been anonymous. He had a tough choice; he made his decision and wrote down the numbers I wanted. From memory too; the old momser knew them, all right.

Then he got out his memo book. I filled in my name and address, he wrote a description of the stones and gave it to me to sign. I pushed it back.

"Weights on the memo, Stony."

He concealed his dislike, very poorly, and put them in. I checked his figures against the scrap of paper, eyed the stones, made sure all information was on both copies, and signed my name.

He gave me my copy and he gave me the merchandise. I admit that I shook hands with him. – Police business!

It was lunchtime when I hit the street. The rain had gone. The sidewalks were jammed, mostly with kibitzers in the trade, each one pursuing some miserable triviality as if a murder depended on it. I was delighted to find that I was hungry. A man with such big deals can't eat in a cheap café, so I walked to the Wentworth and enjoyed a meal I could have afforded if I had sold one of the pellets in my pocket.

I didn't like my position. I was on the point of breaking something. I didn't know what, or what it would do to me.

I couldn't let Marder in on it because he would have grabbed all the hot stuff I had collected, I thought about Rose, wondered what Cassidy was doing, wondered if I was next on the dead list, left the restaurant, and headed for the distinguished house of Bartolomi. I had the goods to show him now; it was time for a finish – with him it would be Florentine.

And I wondered why Schultz wasn't scared any more. He had been as cool as Bartolomi.

XXI

On the way over I went into Blok's place. Herman was in, and I thought he looked relieved when he saw me. What the hell! I had held his merchandise for a week. I gave the goods back to him, thanked him sincerely enough, and asked:

"Herman, has anybody inquired about me?"

"I had a couple of calls, Saul."

"Who?"

"Manny Capple, for one."

I hadn't even mentioned Blok's name to the fat buzzard. "Who else?"

"Stony Schultz."

"Who else?"

"Battista Bartolomi."

"What did they want?"

"Did you represent me."

"What did you tell them?"

"The truth."

"And what was the truth, Herman?"

"That you did."

I squeezed his hand gratefully and left. My father had some loyal friends.

Within ten minutes the established representative of the House of Blok was opening a brass door attached to a famous Madison Avenue jeweler's. A representative of nineteenth-century civilization released the inner door for me. I wondered how such antiques ever got down and picked up a stone if they happened to drop one. Obviously Bartolomi must close the important sales himself; those pensioners couldn't have been trusted with any deal bigger than a pearl catch.

I got upstairs readily enough; there's nothing like leaving large diamonds wherever you go to ensure your re-entry. Bartolomi's office door was open and he sat at the walnut desk. This time he wore a suit of a bluish mixture and he was a symphony in restrained luxury.

"Good evening, Mr. Handy."

He pointed to the chair beside his desk. The tables nearby were littered, as before, with every jewel which comes out of the ground, set into every variety of feminine silliness.

"Are you interested in semiprecious stones?" he asked amiably.

"I don't know much about them."

"They can be very deceiving. With all my experience, I'm often fooled. What would you think this is?"

He handed me an earring which held a medium-sized opaque stone of deep blue-purple. I looked at it uncertainly.

"I would call it lapis lazuli."

He nodded. "It's dyed agate. I wouldn't know without the invoice."

Considering that we had no possible business with each other, we were taking our time. He was inspecting me closely in his offhand, blasé-gentleman style. I was in no hurry either; I would have spent all night with him. Finally he said:

"I can't use the diamond you left with me. I can't reach my prospect. I don't handle loose stones ordinarily, but I had thought I might have an outside sale for this one. But the customer has left for Europe, and it doesn't mean enough to me to work on it further."

This was a big mouthful of nothing since he could have walked into Harry Winston's or the Diamond Club (he was a member) and sold the diamond in five minutes at a thousand-dollar profit. He didn't want that stone; he didn't want any part of it, because he took out the paper and opened it on the desk. The chill brilliant, shaped like a woman, lay flaming in its slick paper – a nude on a

143

bedsheet. I glanced at it and folded the paper without louping it.

"It's a very interesting piece of goods, Mr. Handy," he went on. "Would you mind telling me something of its history?"

"All I know about it," I answered while I watched him, "is the man who gave it to me, and I can't give out his name because he doesn't want the trade to know he needs cash that badly."

"*That* badly," he observed, "is very badly."

"Yes," I agreed, "it is – I'd like to show you a few more."

I took out everything I had and first gave him Capple's stone. He asked the price; I quoted my cost; he pushed it over to me without comment. Then I gave him Moselle's other substitute. He gave it a fast one; I quoted Moselle's cost (Moselle's cost on the missing original, of course). He started to give it back to me, stopped himself, held it for a better look, rotating it slowly, and then slowly laid it down.

"A good buy," he remarked evenly, "but I don't need it."

Now I offered Schultz's two diamonds. He took his quick one, took it slower, gave me a quick one, and put them on the desk between us but not all the way over to me.

"Is your source confidential on these?"

This seemed unnecessary, since I hadn't quoted a price, but I said, "It's the same man."

He seemed to hesitate, a serious businessman in a moment of indecision. Then slowly, "As I said, I don't use these sizes, even though they are good buys."

This meant that he was so sure the goods were cheap that he didn't need to ask the price; that he was sure the stuff was hot and he didn't touch such things. But I had offered him no bargain on Capple's diamond; why should he assume that these two were bargains?

I made my last play. "Look at this one, Mr. Bartolomi. It's not the best but the price takes care of that." I uncovered the pear which had come out of the dead man's room.

His nose went up a little as he noticed its dullness, but

he picked it up. And when he put his glass on it, his steadiness failed him for a second. Only around the mouth, of course, as I watched his bent head, but I wasn't going through all that without keeping my eyes open. When he got tired of looking at it, he laid it down and said:

"Could I ask you to wait outside for a few minutes, Mr. Handy? I would like to make a phone call, and then I'll decide what I can do for you."

He was perfectly convincing. I agreed, as the eager salesman naturally would, and retired to his anteroom. He followed me politely, pointed to a velvet bench along the silver-papered wall, closed the door apologetically, and left me calculating the value of the goods I had left on his desk without witness or receipt. I would be on a lovely spot if he (1) had me thrown out and simply kept the merchandise, (2) called the police, (3) made some fancy switches and waited to see what I would do.

But I didn't think he would do any of those things; as he said, he would make an urgent telephone call and then he would know how to play it.

I waited at least ten minutes during which time I reflected that he probably had a gun not far from all that merchandise. Then the door opened and Bartolomi motioned me in. His manner had changed; there was a studied coldness. He pointed to the desk and said, "I can't use your goods, Mr. Handy."

"But I haven't given you prices."

"At no price."

He was as firm as a banker brushing off an unsound borrower or a businessman of high integrity disdaining to soil his hands with suspicious merchandise. If he were an honest man, he would be doing exactly what he was doing.

I folded up my goods without using a glass. After my hands were empty, I looked him in the eye.

"What's wrong, Mr. Bartolomi? Talking to your prospect seems to have made a big difference."

"No difference, Mr. Handy. I'm going to be very busy now."

I nodded. We kept our hands at our sides. I walked to the narrow stairs beside the little elevator. He stood in his doorway and watched me start down the steps. No Florentine robber-prince ever looked finer, harder, or more masterful. The silver-papered wall made a frame around him; all he needed was a piece of ermine over the shoulder and an executioner in the shadows.

The relic was on duty at the entrance. I noticed two employees, one a woman. As usual, no customers. The door opened for me, I lingered between the two brass doors long enough to think what a lovely place it would be for a murder, and departed from the Palazzo Bartolomi.

I did everything short of trotting to get back to the Street of Memos and that jewel, Schultz. I had to ring his bell, of course, to go through the waiting room, which was a pity, since I would have given a quarter-carat imperfect to have heard a bit of the telephone conversation Stony was sweating out. He hung up, came out mumbling, jumped half out of his speckled skin when he saw me, and said wildly:

"Saul – glad you showed – need those diamonds right away – got a hot prospect."

He actually held out his hands in the doorway as if I were palming them. I stared at him without a word.

"Got to have them, Saul. I was going wild! Big deal. Chance to make something. What a break! – Gimme 'em."

I pushed slowly into his office and up to his desk, he weaving backward and forward in uncertain little jerks. I sat down and looked up at him. His skin was like dirty white blotting paper, his mouth was trembling and wet, and he was breathing with a break in the gas line.

"What's all this about, Stony?" I asked in tones of soft wonder. "Who's the hot prospect – a Texas oilman?"

"A Texas oilman. . . . What's Texas got to do with it? I need them right away. Got to go to his hotel. Millionaire from Chicago. Boy, is he loaded! Big spender. Act at once. Go to his hotel. Waldorf. Leaves tonight–"

"For Hong Kong?"

"Hong Kong! What are you asking me that for? Trying to cut in on me, Saul, old boy? Come on, give me the stuff. Here's your memos."

He grabbed his memo book and tore my sheet out of it. And I mean tore; he tore it in half.

"Stony,"I said gently, "I can't give you the diamonds today. I left them with my customer."

He screamed. "Saul, don't go cute on me! Look, Saul, I gotta have that goods. I'll give you a cut on my deal, Saul old boy, a cool hundred for you—"

He pulled out his wallet and started to count out tens and twenties.

I said, "Don't you hear me, Stony? I haven't got them on me."

"You're lying. Where did you leave them? Go after them, Saul — I'll go with you. A hundred dollars clear for you to pay for your trouble. Let's go." He seized his hat and pulled it down on his head.

"Stony," I said without moving, "we can't get them today any more. We simply can't. I'll get them tomorrow if my customer doesn't want them. One you can surely have; he won't sell both. Tomorrow."

"Saul, are you trying to drive me crazy? Give me my merchandise!"

"You don't understand, Stony. I can't pressure my customer — you just don't try it with this guy. He's a big operator. Tomorrow."

"*Who's got them?*"

"Battista Bartolomi."

His head wobbled on his chicken's neck. The eyes expanded, a shiver went through him, he stared stupidly at me, looked at the phone, started to dial, stopped, and cried hoarsely, "You mean it, Saul?" and went on dialing. He didn't look up any telephone number; when a voice came through the wires, he croaked, "Mr. Bartolomi, — Mr. Schultz. Schultz Importing . . . Mr. Bartolomi, Mr. Handy tells me that you have two diamonds of mine in your possession. I . . . He's here in my office . . . on memo, he says. . . . Why would he say it? . . ."

He hung up.

I said,"What did he say?"

He was almost cool now. "You never left them."

I said, "Did you expect him to admit it?"

"You've got them on you."

I said, "He knows they're hot. He'd be crazy to admit he had them."

"*Give me my diamonds, Saul.*"

I stood up. He was only a little old man, but he, too, might have a gun somewhere. "I can't, Stony. Tomorrow I'll get them from Bartolomi. Tomorrow morning. *I* don't want them. Sorry."

We stood measuring each other, he calm as despair, I a picture of an apologetic salesman who has pulled a boner.

It was time to go; I couldn't be sure that the trouble shooters weren't coming. I reached sidewise for the door and pulled it open. The two setters were at their benches.

"See you tomorrow, Stony. Stop worrying so much; Battista Bartolomi can be depended upon. You can trust him to do anything he says he'll do." I went through the door and through the two outer doors as if I were on well-greased roller skates, and I tripped lightly down the stairs. There was the burglar alarm running up the door frame and I felt like a burglar, but I wasn't afraid anybody would call the cops.

I had them rolling.

XXII

It was still getting colder; the bite of October felt good blowing the Schultz off me. I waited a moment, crossed the street to the Wentworth, and phoned Moselle's Exchange.

"I'd like to see you as soon as possible, Barney?"

"Here?"

"No."

"I can be home in twenty minutes."

"I'll be there."

I took a quick one at the bar, hailed a cab going up Sixth Avenue, and enjoyed fifteen minutes of riding through the dusk. We circled the park, pulled up in front of that stately apartment house, and I entered the confluence of the self-made rich.

Lila answered the door; she stood looking at me gravely, showing neither welcome nor unfriendliness. She wore a housecoat, all crimson and gold. Her black hair and black eyes gleamed; the perfect oval of her face was intensified by her pale white skin. The whole woman was redolent of luxury, self-control, and innate dignity. It seemed inconceivable that this beauty had writhed wildly on my lap just one day ago.

I said, "Barney must be right behind me. We have business to take care of."

"Come in, Saul."

She stepped aside and I went through the foyer into the big room.

"Please sit down." She motioned me toward the chair I had used on my first visit. She sat in the corresponding place partly facing me. She asked quietly, "You know about Raphael?"

"Yes."

"What do you think?"

"What is there to think?"

"Why?" She looked at me intently. "Why? What reason?"

"I don't know."

"Did that woman do it?"

"The waitress?" I said. "How could I know? Why would she?"

"Love?"

"Did she love him? – It's not a characteristic woman's killing. Women seldom club people."

She shuddered. It seemed to be a true shudder, not a conventional gesture. Indeed, I never had seen Lila express conventional emotion.

She said, "The papers make everything so horrible. How are you making out?"

"Not too bad."

"Do you think you can wind things up soon?"

"Possibly."

"I hope so. Barney has been under so much strain lately."

"He has? Why?"

Her eyes were serious. "Isn't it natural under the circumstances?"

"It depends. I don't know much of his personal business."

She colored. "Too much perhaps. More than you should."

"I don't think so," I said with gravity equal to her own.

"It depends on what one calls personal business and what one thinks is too much."

I leaned forward, not forgetting however that Barney would walk in at any moment. "You, Lila, would be too much, I think, for any man."

Then the door did open and the overtaxed husband came in, tall, gray, pink, but not looking any younger. Lila rose, they kissed, how are you, dear? tired darling? hello Saul, hello Barney, have some brandy, Saul.

Saul would, Barney would, Lila no.

"Can you stay for dinner?"

"I can't, Mrs. Moselle. I must work on some things tonight."

He said, "We'd better go into the study. Excuse us, dear."

"Only for a little while. Take the brandy with you."

We settled down in the office-den, Barney behind his desk, I alongside it. I took out the diamond papers and laid his goods on the desk.

"Check them in, Barney. I'm through with them. I'm sure there's been no substitutions, but here are the microphotographs if you want to check. Take very good care of everything. I'm positive one is stolen."

He did seem tired. "How can you be sure?"

"It's been recognized. At least two people spotted it."

"Who?"

"Stony Schultz, for one."

"I'm not surprised. Who's the other?"

"Battista Bartolomi."

This time he reacted. He gave me a look, took out his glass, louped the hot one quickly, and sighed.

"It's a big loss. Three of them. But surely not Bartolomi."

"Surely Bartolomi."

"The man's credit is tops."

"Don't trust it. It won't be for long."

"You're certain you know what you're doing?"

"I'm certain I know what I'm saying. Doing is another matter."

"Battista is an old friend of my wife's."

"So she told me."

He was surprised. "When?"

"The last time I was here."

He nodded. "She did many pieces for him. That's how I met her; they needed one of my emeralds. Battista didn't do so good on that deal. Before we were done, I had given Lila the emerald and taken her for my wife."

"She was worth it."

"She was. But I'd hate to be the cause of trouble coming

151

to Battista. I would have to be absolutely sure, and then sure that it was necessary.

"I am beginning to think, Barney, that Barolomi is the biggest fence in America. Did you ever see these?" I rolled out Schultz's two diamonds.

He picked them up, one at a time, and delicately examined the stones. His hands were exquisite, big though he was, as he rotated the marquise in his tweezers.

He laid the diamonds in their papers. "Never saw them before. Whose are they?"

"Schultz's."

"Nice goods."

"At $1,400 per carat?"

He nodded slowly. "That's what Schultz asks?"

"That's all. They're yours if you want them."

"I'll pass."

"So did Bartolomi. But not because they were too cheap."

"Why?"

"Because they were his already. He was selling, not buying." I took out the diamond Bender had lent me. "Ever seen this?"

He gave it a quickie. "I don't think so."

"I'm glad to hear that."

The phone rang. Moselle answered and held out the receiver. "For you."

I mouthed noiselessly, "Me?"

He nodded.

"How?" (In the same way.)

He shrugged. I took the instrument as if it were as hot as those diamonds.

"Handy speaking."

An unmistakable voice, slimy as old plumbing, put a dank chill into the room.

"Saul boy, I've got to see you."

My mind was sorting out answers like an electronic computer. "You'll see me tomorrow, Stony. I told you that."

"No. Tonight."

152

"What good would tonight do you? I can't see Bartolomi until tomorrow."

"Stop horsing me, Saul. Saul boy, you see me tonight and give me my diamonds, I'll tell you something you want to know. Something you want bad."

I was pacing my breathing. "Like what, Stony? What do I want bad?"

A whisper crawled along the line. "Like Raphael D'Arle. Like Idaho."

I held the receiver, staring blankly at Moselle and trying to fit motives.

"Interested, Saul boy?"

"I think I am, Stony."

"Right away?"

I hadn't made the connections. I said cautiously, "No hurry. I'm tied up. Why not tomorrow morning?"

"Won't do. Gotta be tonight."

What the hell. I didn't know what I was doing anyhow. "Make it ten o'clock."

"Here?"

"Where the hell are you?"

"In my place." The voice had gone up to an indignant whine.

"O.K. your place. Ten o'clock."

"No horsing now, Saul. You ain't giving me the runaround?"

"Ten o'clock, you greasy old bastard. It better be good."

He hung up. I did the same after a minute. Moselle and I sat looking across the desk. He said:

"Bartolomi again?"

"Oh, yes. By all means. Bartolomi again."

"Bartolomi has something of yours?"

"Oh, no. I have something of his." I put Schultz's diamonds in my pocket.

He asked, "Will you give those back to Schultz?"

"Why not? I signed a memo."

"But they're stolen."

"Sometimes it takes one to catch one. I don't know they're stolen."

"I do," he remarked amiably.

153

"Just distress merchandise, Barney. Somebody needs cash in a hurry."

He shrugged his heavy shoulders. "I'm sorry about Battista. He was at our wedding. He's in the wedding pictures."

My spine became alive with little whispers. "You have a picture of him?"

"Of course."

"In this room?"

He looked at me blankly. "Yes, I think I do."

"Can I see it?"

He got up, went to his filing cabinet, ran over some folders, and took one out. "He's in here some place."

My hand shook when I reached for the folder. It held the usual collections of photos, taken in one of the big hotel ballrooms: guests, the bridal couple (Moselle a little younger, Lila looking exactly as she had looked an hour ago), a number of candid shots of the party and the dancing, and a group picture of Moselle, Lila, Bartolomi, and a fat blond man whom I recognized as Jan Van Vliet, no less – it was the aristocracy of the jewelry world.

"No relatives?"

"None present. Lila hasn't a soul. Her only sister died many years ago."

"Could I have this one for a few days, Barney?"

"What on earth will you do with it? Do you think you can pin something on Van Vliet?"

I smiled quite gaily, quite candidly. "Maybe on you, Barney – I'll take good care of it."

"I have duplicates." He sighed at the picture. "The years, Saul, the years!"

"It's only about five years, isn't it?"

"Just passed. Five years last May."

I got up and held out Bender's stone. "Put this in a safe place, Barney. It's important that I don't lose it."

He saw me to the door. Lila was not in sight. Maybe she was cooking his dinner with those trained, fastidious hands; I hadn't seen a servant.

I went back to my hotel room; why I didn't know. I sat in that miserable hole twiddling Schultz's diamond papers.

Since that gave me no inspiration, I took down a suitcase which I kept locked on the shelf of my moldy closet and examimined my old, licensed, legal, forbidden, other .38. I hadn't thought it necessary to explain to Cassidy that I had two revolvers. And of course he hadn't checked; he only took the first gun to annoy me.

It was loaded. I removed the cartridges, worked the trigger a few times, decided it would still do if only to hang me by, reloaded it, checked the safety, and dropped it into my pants pocket where it lay like a thousand pennyweight.

I then did get a kind of idea. I phoned a Westchester address. Another cool, controlled, well-rounded voice answered.

"This is Saul Handy. Is Mr. Bender at home?"

Out of cracking ice: "I'll see, Mr. Handy."

In a minute, a half snarl, "Yes?"

"The souvenir you loaned me this morning–"

"Well?"

"It's been recognized."

A savage whisper, "Cops?"

"If cops, I wouldn't be calling. By a fence."

"Where is it now?"

"Safe. But I think the police will have to get it sooner or later."

The whisper was softer, "If like from me, Handy, you won't enjoy the joke."

"Stop chilling my blood. I told you, not from you. One thing–"

"Yes?"

"You're positive you're not in on any blunt instrument killings?"

"Why are you asking now?"

"Because if you're not, that's a green light."

"It's green. Is that why you called?"

"And to know if you know a man named Schultz."

"Who's Schultz?"

"A guy who's supposed to know about a New York abstract expressionist."

Silence. . . . "When will you know what he knows?"

"Tonight – if he's leveling."

155

"Up to midnight, phone me."

"If I'm alive."

We hung up.

I had promised to call Marder. I phoned. Sergeant Bramson answered. Marder had gone home, for once. This Bramson hadn't been such a bad guy; I asked him if the name Schultz of Forty-seventh Street meant anything to the jewelry detail. It didn't, so far as he knew. Handy meant something, he assured me. He also told me the New York police have no jewelry detail. They were part of burglary. I told him I would call the lieutenant tomorrow.

So I went outdoors. The Champlain was no longer crowded. I had duck with orange slices, which tasted like duck without orange slices, and a large glass of their cheapest white wine. It was 9:20. I decided I didn't need to respect Schultz's appointment book any closer. I paid the cashier and the coat-check girl, wriggled past an incoming parcel of people with *out-of-town* all over them, and headed for Forty-seventh Street – Forty-seventh Street, where the sheep come to get gold cheap – Forty-seventh Street.

XXIII

The block was lonely, a black Tundra, when I hammered on the outside door. There was no answer but it was unlocked; no great wonder since the Holmes protection took care of every opening on the floor above. The old fire-trap was dark inside though; I hadn't expected that, and I would have stopped then and there, but I could see light from Schultz's office window shining yellowishly into the street. I went up carefully since all I had to see by came from underneath the steel door on the second floor, wondering how Schultz knew, when he came down those stairs, that there wouldn't be a thug waiting for him at the foot.

There was no outside bell. I pounded in the darkness with my fist. Nothing stirred. I was half an hour early, but if he wasn't there, the downstairs door should have been locked. Also he wouldn't leave the place without setting the alarm and then he couldn't come back. So I banged and banged and kicked the door, and I remembered my gun, so I took it out and banged with the handle, and it made a big noise.

Nobody but an idiot would sit in a lonely office surrounded by jewelry and leave the door unlocked. Still, I tried it and when it came open, letting light into the hall, something had to be wrong. So I pointed my gun in front of me and swung it in a short arc and heard a stirring *outside* the door, near me, on the landing. I spun partly around with my gun pointed out, but too slow. A murderous blow came down on my shoulder – my left shoulder, not the side that held the gun – and I stood paralyzed, slumping gently, my forehead rubbing along the wall; but still I heard someone go down the steps, sick as I was and blind with pain.

Nothing moved. I thought I never would. My breath came in like tearing wounds, and I couldn't tell where I was hurt. I was a heap on the floor, half sitting, I suppose, my forehead resting. I was waiting, I think, to die.

But that didn't come. In time I got myself on my hands and knees, and climbed up on the wall and let the light from the door beat on my eyes. I thought of my gun; I still had it. I had never let go. I hadn't shot myself or anybody else; I had never taken off the safety. I hadn't the will to take it off now; I put the useless weight back in my pocket and stepped into the tiny vestibule.

The door to the inside was open. I started to go in; my senses came back to me. I reached my good arm inside the door and squeezed the alarm, which ran along the doorpost, handy for anybody looking out the peephole. Handy for Handy, too; I didn't go to the next door, which led into Schultz's office. Instead I staggered out of the waiting room and down the stairs and reeled toward Fifth Avenue, into the one-way traffic if there should be any, but away from the point the Holmes men come from.

And I didn't stop staggering until I had reached the steps of the public library at Forty-second Street, six blocks away. I sat on the stone steps near the lions and waited for my world to come back.

After a while I could move my arm, and I could shrug my shoulder. Nothing was broken or not too badly. Since I had come that far, I got up and made the curb too, and, in time, made a taxi.

Dressed as I was and the way I felt, I told the driver to make it Idlewild. The cabby looked closely at me; I couldn't blame him, for such a long ride, so I got my hand into my pocket and showed him I had money.

I must have passed out because I came to when his hand shook my bad shoulder – I thought I was back on that landing.

I had no reservations and no exact idea how to get to where I wanted. A brutal throbbing shrunk my stomach at timed intervals – maybe every five seconds. I had no change of clothes, and barely enough money for a one-way ticket.

I couldn't get a plane that would move me in the right direction sooner than four hours. So I took what ticket I could get and found a bar with tables, not too crowded at that hour, and I sat and drank my whiskies, nursing them fearfully, because I didn't dare lose consciousness. I swallowed two aspirins each hour. After three hours, I got up, drunk enough to explain my weaving, found the airport washroom, washed up, and felt better. When I could, around three in the morning, I got tucked into my seat, felt the plane move in my shoulder as real as if it were pulling me, and when the little girl came around I asked for black coffee.

I slept the sad, broken, heavy sleep of the sick for most of the flight. A wonderful sun was preparing to rise over the mountains as we came into Denver. I had no time to enjoy it. I had a tight schedule, but we made connections, and I took off toward the north country. The mountains shrank, the sun rose higher, we went down into the valley and landed neatly on the airport at Boise. I taxied frantically for the bus terminal. Half an hour later I was riding along the valley floor, then up over a broad divide, down again through unending acres of what had been potato fields last summer; and we pulled into a pretty little town, windy and sun-drenched, sticking on a flat plateau.

I was in Muskingdon, Idaho.

I thought I might need two days. I found Western Union, wired the Corbin's for $200 and not to talk about it, found a hotel (not bad, big room), took a very hot bath, and located a doctor.

He was a shrewd old guy, much like Dr. Stimson in Springfield, and I didn't try to tell him I had had a fall. I said I had been slugged in Chicago, and since anything goes if you blame it on Chicago, he didn't stop to check whether I was wanted.

I didn't know if I was wanted myself. There was no possible connection between any bodies found in Schultz's office and me (if there were any bodies in Schultz's office), excepting (1) Moselle knew I was seeing Schultz; (2)

Bramson had a lead, unfortunately, which would come up sooner or later; (3) Bender had heard me use Schultz's name; (4) the Corbin's knew, now, that I was in Muskingdon. They wouldn't talk unless homicide came around, but I couldn't ask them to obstruct police business. Not murder business.

Of course, there might have been no murder.

The doctor strapped up my shoulder, gave me a shot and some pills, and advised a few days in bed. It was good advice; I put the pills in my pocket and started for the offices of the *Idaho Advocate*.

The *Advocate* was a daily. How these small-town papers hang on, I do not know; but many of them apparently continue enlightening five or ten thousand families, keeping them up-to-date on the deaths of local lizards and the births of local colts, just as they did when my father was born. The *Advocate* (whose platform is more prosperity) showed one girl and, in the background, a kind of printing press. Any men, presumably, were out digging up whatever news lay buried under the chill sun. The girl was about thirty-two and not bad in a potato-field sort of way.

"Howdy, stranger," I began. I was thrilled at the way my Illinois intonation came back to me.

She leaned across the yellow-oak rail separating the office from the reception space and scanned my collar.

"Brush off that potato bug," she suggested. "You'll have to watch for things like that if you want to visit the big city."

"I do feel kinda lost," I said, "all these crowds and everything. Why do they rush so?"

"The only rushes I notice," she said, "are bull-rushes."

I grinned at her. "I can see that we are going to get along. I'm lucky to have found a girl like you right away, who will be delighted to help me."

"You probably are. In what way, strictly connected with running a newspaper, can I be of help to you?"

"You can search your memory for faces." I took out the wedding picture. "Do you know any of these?"

She studied the photo, frowning slightly, and I thought I saw her face change. She lowered the picture.

160

"Who are you?"

"My name is Saul Handy." There was no use trying to hide anything; I needed my identity to collect Corbin's money at the telegraph office.

She had never heard of me. "What is your interest in these people?"

"A very serious one. You do recognize somebody?"

"I might."

I turned the picture slightly and pointed to Barolomi. "Him?"

"No."

I smiled into her eyes and it was my best smile. "Then I want you to tell me one thing and show me one thing."

"What?"

"Her name, and what issues of the paper I should look in for her."

"You don't know her name?"

"I know her as Lila."

"So do I." She was searching something in my face. "If you know that much you can find the rest. Are you a lawyer?"

"A private detective. Formerly with the Chicago police force."

"You don't know her last name?"

"Moselle. Born Lila Dumont."

"Dufort," she corrected. "She's the last of them. There's not too much in the paper. What do you want to know?"

I told her. We had a quiet talk and looked over a few old issues. I left.

The Corbins had come through at Western Union: money and a message. *Rough night on lapidaries*, it read. *Blunt.*

My reflexes very blunt, I signed for the money. The sheriff was not around. I walked to the bus station, bought a ticket, left within forty minutes, and made my planes at Boise and Denver – a busy day.

XXIV

Idlewild hadn't changed: it was still cold and dark. Cassidy wasn't there; in fact nobody cared who got off that plane at six in the morning. I told a cab driver to go to police headquarters, Manhattan, and closed my eyes for a few minutes of half-sleep.

After a while I lifted my bruised body out of the cab and forced myself to walk into that building again. I was still wearing the clothes I had been slugged in, and when I asked for Marder I half expected to be sent to the delousing room.

I got him, though, two hours later, and his cohorts; Marder looking more hatchet-faced, hook-nosed, chin-hooked than ever.

"Me, you want?" he began.

"Who else?"

"We have so many departments: arson, vice, fraud, narcotics . . ."

"Homicide?"

"Oh, yes, homicide."

"I don't want them."

"Strange. I'm sure they want you."

"Before you verify that, lieutenant, I think you should listen to a few details concerning your own department."

"My pleasure. Shall we use my office?"

"It would be more relaxing there."

He led the way, Druckman and Bramson coming after me. It was a nice, spacious office, big enough for a captain.

"Sit right down and fall apart," he said.

"We'll put you together again," Druckman contributed.

I sat, felt the chill bite of extreme exhaustion, and asked

for coffee. I did not want them to find out that my shoulder hurt me; *that* probably would have got me a murder rap.

I began, "I would like to get Barney Moselle down here as fast as possible. Try this number and let me talk to him, please."

Druckman said, "I wouldn't keep Mr. Handy waiting, Lieutenant."

They found Barney at home quick enough.

"Where have you been, Saul?" Moselle asked.

"Here and there. I'll tell you when you get here."

"Where are you?"

"Police headquarters. I'd like you to come down at once and bring the three diamonds with you; the two you found and the one I gave you. You've kept them in the house, haven't you?"

"Yes. Must it be now?"

"I'm afraid so, Barney. The police won't wait."

"Have you accomplished anything?"

"I think it's over, as far as you are concerned."

"I'll start right away."

I hung up. Marder was drumming the table.

"Talk," he said.

I talked. I told him everything and at length about Moselle's memo list, about Herman Blok, Stony Schultz, and Bartolomi. I pronounced Schultz's name without change of pitch or tempo. I discussed Moselle's suspected stones and the microphotos. I did *not* mention that I had gone back to Schultz's place that night.

When I stopped, Druckman said, "That's one great big heap for the cleaning woman."

"Wait for Moselle," I replied. "I'll tie it up. In the meantime, look at these." I took out Schultz's diamonds and gave them to Marder. "Maybe you know them."

He gave the stones a fast one with his glass. He knew goods, all right; some guys take to it better than others; I never would understand merchandise the way he did.

"Well?" I asked.

"Maybe I know them."

"By sight or by reputation?"

"Maybe by reputation."

163

"So?"

"So, suppose you tell us where you got them," he snarled. His eyes were hostile too.

I gave him my copy of Schultz's memo. They gathered around that piece of paper and then waited for me.

"These are the two stones," I said, "that Bartolomi ran away from and that Schultz had to get back."

Marder put them under a low-powered microscope, then went to his files, made some notes, folded the diamonds in thin papers, and put them in his safe.

"I'll have to return them to Schultz," I pointed out.

"What a wise guy," Druckman said. "Some wise guy."

"*That's* for Cassidy," Marder said. "You admit these came from Schultz."

"I allege it."

"What happened," Bramson asked, "after you phoned me? What happened between you and Schultz?"

"I haven't seen Schultz since then," I answered truthfully. "The last I saw Schultz was around five o'clock the day before yesterday, and the last time I heard from him was in Moselle's home, an hour or so later, when he phoned me."

"And made an appointment." Bramson was no dope. "What happened at your appointment?"

"I couldn't keep it," I said still quite truthful. "I had to leave town."

"Where to?"

"Let's hold that back until Moselle gets here," I suggested. "It's no secret but I have my reasons for waiting."

"Did you fly?" Marder asked.

"Yes."

"It wouldn't be Idaho?"

I looked at him. "Yes, it would, lieutenant. But for the next twenty-four hours can we keep that strictly to ourselves?"

"Between us cops," Druckman said bitterly. "May we tell homicide, Officer Handy?"

"I wouldn't tell homicide anything if I were you until you get what you need out of me."

164

It still seems a harmless remark to me, but Druckman got up quickly and grabbed my shoulder – the bad one, of couse. The room turned over, I half rose unsteadily, and then fell back into my chair. They all looked surprised.

"Are you sick?" Marder asked.

"I'm not so good. Do you have any aspirin?"

He opened a drawer and shoved a bottle at me. I took two tablets with some cold coffee and sat trembling, as much from fear as from pain. Two minutes more and they would have got the rest of it, but Moselle came in. I saw that tall, tired, gray-haired, pink-skinned man and snapped back.

We shook hands; Moselle took out three papers and exposed the three stones on the desk. Marder let them lie. "What's the story?"

"These two," I said, pointing, "turned up in Moselle's stock. He thinks they are substitutes, presumably for goods let out on consignment. Including the Israeli stone, that makes three switches. I know they're hot. Can you identify them?"

Marder pointed to Bender's dull beauty. "This one?"

"Nothing to do with Mr. Moselle. Somebody else gave it to me."

"Come on. Who?"

"I agreed to keep my source confidential."

"That don't go, Handy, and you know it."

"It'll go unless you can identify it."

He took about twenty minutes. He louped the stones carefully, made notes on each one, put them under the microscope, took more papers out of his file, put Moselle's stones in envelopes, wrote on the envelopes, and put them in the safe. Then he turned to me, with Bender's diamond in his hand.

"I can identify it. Who?"

"Al Light."

They blinked at me as if they were actors in a TV science fiction story. "You held out this envelope from a murder investigation?"

"No," I answered politely, "you have not correctly described the event."

165

"When did Light give it to you?"

"He didn't"

"How did you get it?"

"I understand it was found in his apartment."

"And who gave you to understand?"

I inhaled gently. "It was given to me by a messenger. It came in a plain blank envelope. Then I got a phone call suggesting that I look into the matter. The voice, a man's, said that it was from Light's place. That's all I know."

"When?"

"The day before yesterday."

"Where's the envelope?"

"I may have it in my room."

"He may," Bramson said.

"Should we get a search warrant?" Druckman asked.

"Hell, no," I said. "I'll help you look, but you won't find prints on that envelope. Except mine."

"Except his," Druckman agreed.

Marder said, "Let's add up this bunch of half-truths, whole lies, palpable evasions, and unsubstantiated insinuations. You say that Battista Bartolomi is a master fence for stolen and smuggled goods. You claim he got rid of the stuff by exchanging it with clean goods taken on consignment, working through Schultz and presumably others, and by mounting the stolen merchandise into pieces imported from Italy—"

"And no doubt by means of an occasional private sale, and, for ordinary routine stuff, by straight sales over his counters. And sometimes by recutting, of course."

"How much could he get rid of that way?"

"I don't know how much business he does," I said. "But if he does two million a year on paper, he could unload a million dollars' worth of hot goods."

Marder said thoughtfully, "It would be a big operation. How the hell do we prove some of it?"

"You can't. Not you alone. You'll have to use the Feds."

"On what grounds?"

"There is a weakness in Bartolomi's position. One way or the other, he's getting in more goods than he can show invoices for. He's got to sell this goods openly, or secretly, or keep it somewhere in the form of a hoard of precious stones. Your best move is to investigate the possibility that he has sold too much merchandise. That would mean that his paid federal luxury taxes would be too large for his purchases. Also his luxury taxes would be too large for his income taxes."

"I don't see that."

"It's simple enough. He gets stones on memo, say, for $10,000. He replaces them with $10,000 worth of stolen goods, or even $12,000 worth. What does he care as long as he keeps the stuff moving?

"Now he's got $10,000 in clean goods but he must turn the clean stuff into money fast so he can continue the operation. After all, he may need $100,000 any night, maybe three o'clock in the morning, to handle some sudden haul.

"So he sells the clean goods *below* proper retail price, showing little or no profit, or even a loss. He presumably is smart enough to keep a clean set of books, so he pays his 10 per cent luxury tax to Uncle Sam. He pays on every sale. He fakes a cost, of course, for every item he sells, but he surely isn't going to fake a low cost, because then his income tax will shoot up. So he makes the sales show a small profit on paper and he has a small income tax compared to his big luxury taxes. He keeps on doing a big business, but he never makes any money."

Marder began to look like a man hunter. He said, "Or else he holds out on his luxury tax to make his income tax look reasonable."

"Or else," I said, "he has a bank roll somewhere which he doesn't report at all."

"Or else he has a safe full of diamonds that he can't explain. But this is guesswork."

"Not entirely. You do have him as a Moselle customer. I've seen him going into Schultz's place. You have Schultz as a Moselle customer. And you have the Warrington cop-killing. The Treasury boys will listen to you for enough to start a tax investigation. The FBI will work on the cop-killing. New York City will work on his city sales tax. — That's an awful lot of pressure on a man who is all front.

167

Don't forget he's very vulnerable. He's all prestige, front, bluff. The minute he becomes hot, the underworld will drop him."

"And we might have a bit of luck," Marder said thoughtfully.

"That's it. You may find some hot merchandise. After that, let the tax boys work on his purchases. Find out why he brings in so much Italian goods just to lose money on it. I'll bet my life he doesn't show a real profit for the past ten years."

"Your life," said Marder affably, "I almost forgot. Call homicide, Druckman."

Druckman smiled happily and spoke into the phone. We sat and waited, Marder sunk in a cop's reverie, Moselle baffled and unhappy, Druckman and Bramson impassive, I too tired to care.

Moselle asked, "Where have you been, Saul?"

"Wyoming," I answered.

Three cops never blinked. "Wyoming," Moselle said, "that's Lila's home state."

"Is that so?" I said. "She must be a real small-town girl."

"Almost a farmer, I understand. She's going to be upset about Battista."

Marder was watching him now. "Don't tell her," I said. "Don't tell her under any condition. We have no case yet, and we may never have, so she may be spared the whole business. If you tell her, she might let something fall that would warn Bartolomi. It could even involve her."

Marder said, "Don't disclose any part of what you have heard here, Mr. Moselle. Don't mention Bartolomi, Handy, or Wyoming."

"Has Wyoming got anything to do with Bartolomi?"

"Why else would I go out there?" I asked.

He nodded. The policemen never stirred. I dozed for a minute.

Cassidy came in.

His red face was as angry as a face can get. He scanned the office and his eyes came to rest on Marder.

"How long have you had this fugitive?"

"About an hour," Marder answered gently. "Long enough to get Mr. Moselle here."

"Getting Mr. Moselle comes before homicide?"

"Handy came in of his own free will, sergeant. – He's hardly a fugitive. Naturally you want him for questioning."

"Naturally. Naturally, lieutenant."

"You don't have an alarm out on him?"

"Don't I? – Since 6 P.M.

"I missed it, sergeant. I'm supposed to be off duty – since six o'clock. Look, the man came in and has been spitting his guts about a lot of jewelry detail business. If he's spilling it straight, he may have been of some help to us. We've made notes. Some of it bears on your cases. He's all yours now. I'd like a statement later, but that can wait. I didn't see any harm in letting him talk."

"Especially," I cut in, "if what I give you leads to the Warrington killings."

"That's pretty farfetched," Marder said.

"It's damn close. If you get enough on Bartolomi to loosen him up, he can put the finger on more crime than you would know what to do with."

Marder got up. "I'm going home. Let me know what you do with this lone wolf, sergeant. If he's killed anybody, his testimony won't be worth much."

Cassidy wasn't buying peace pipes. "This way, Handy," he said harshly. "We'll do the rest of the talking in a room that ain't so fancy."

Moselle asked carefully, "What are they talking about, Saul – killing somebody?"

"I can't imagine," I answered; "McKinley perhaps."

"Should I speak to my lawyer?"

"Thanks, Barney, I won't need him." I looked at Cassidy. "A doctor maybe – I'll speak to you tomorrow."

"I hope you're right," Moselle said uncertainly.

So did I.

XXV

Cassidy, his ghost, and a third homicide man sweated out a bitter day; a sweating that lasted until almost nine that night. It was a very unsatisfactory way to spend a day. I told them every little thing I knew except that I had been slugged and what I had learned in Idaho.

"You got to Schultz's place," Cassidy repeated for the tenth time. "You were early. The downstairs door was unlocked. You were not surprised. It was dark inside. You went upstairs. So far I might believe you. – Now, *what did you do?*"

And I repeated back, "His door was unlocked with the light on. That didn't make sense. I figured he might have had company waiting for me. Remember, sergeant, he was up to his neck in crime and maybe murder. I reached inside the door, squeezed the alarm, and ran."

That monstrous big head hung over me. "You squeezed the alarm for no reason at all. And then you rushed to Idlewild, took a plane without packing a bag, went to Idaho, also for no reason at all and without stopping to get money, wired the Corbins for $200, checked up on D'Arle and Light although you knew we had all that, flew back – all this time not dreaming that the police were looking for you, not dreaming that Schultz had a smashed head, the third battered skull you've been next to – and then you came back, came right in here, early as it was, for a talk with the jewelry boys – and were you surprised to hear I wanted to talk to you! It don't go down, Handy; you're a dirty, stinking liar; I'm booking you on suspicion of murder."

"What for, sergeant?" I said quietly. "How can it stick?

170

There is no tie-up at all between me and Schultz's killing. Where's the motive? If you had found *my* body, you could hold Schultz. There'd be a motive, maybe. But why would I kill Schultz?"

"You ran away from the scene of the crime."

"How could I know there was a crime?"

"The jury will find the answer."

"Cassidy, do you believe I killed Schultz?"

"You're holding out."

I said, "I will admit one thing: I didn't like the smell of things when I found that door unlocked. There were only two possibilities: one, that I was supposed to walk into a trap and, two, that the boys had closed Schultz's mouth. It very well could have been both. Schultz may have been dead when I got there and they waiting for me, or they may have killed him when I ran and cleared out after me. They may have even planned it that I should go in and be the fall guy."

"And then you went to Idaho."

So it went. I got out at three in the morning. He must have figured that I would lead him to something.

I agreed not to leave town under any condition. Cassidy did let me have one thing: they were not holding Rose. They had let her go after twenty-four hours in the hospital. What had become of her he neither knew nor cared.

I went back to my hotel, left a 9 A.M. call, got into bed, and rejected, temporarily, this stinking world.

The desk clerk's bell fetched me back from farther than Idaho. It was 9:01; the sun shone bright on my carpeting. I took a shower, letting the hot water beat my shoulder for ten minutes. I had a blue-brown patch from my ear to the bottom of my ribs, but I could move more easily, and I felt like myself, for what that was worth. I put on my second-best suit and an aggressive tweed topcoat, and went down for breakfast. After which I reported for work.

It was about 10 A.M. Corbin's was busy, which meant that the fall season was already under way. I went behind the counters with no more than a good morning and a hi-ya, Saul, and started a customer. It was Abe Yamaka; his nauseous personality tasted good after what I had been meeting lately.

He wanted a cultured pearl drop, complete with chain, $1.90 and on memo at that. I gave it to him and kept on taking them as they came, telephone and all, like a man whose only relations with the police were through his wife's father.

—No, that's all the brooches we have — they're all shock-proof, if you don't drop 'em. Maybe the escape wheel is touching the yoke bridge — *Murray, do you have a five ligne* — you'll have to send it back to Providence, we don't service Speidels — Yes, you can have any color stone you want, but it will take one day. — *Jake, can we fit a movement to this case?* — I can't fill this order over the phone until you send a deposit. You can put any ornament we have on any disk, but we can't buy special castings — two carats for $800 and you ask if it's perfect? Bring it back if it don't appraise high enough; no sale's final here. — Madame, there is almost a carat of goods in that piece for one thirty-five, how can you go wrong? — We don't sell by the pennyweight, Ramón, it leads to too much useless talk. — Let's go Max, I'm crowding up. — *Murray, can we furnish a turquoise catch by tomorrow?* Are you going to do the stringing? — gold rope weighs, honey, you can't get a bracelet with rope under $50 unless you use machine-made rope. — We don't have black onyx for women. — *Can you take the phone, Jake, the Jewelers Board of Trade.* — Look Irving, I'm handling three now; I can't walk away from these rings. — The amethysts are genuine; the rubies synthetic of course. — Let me see some identification; this is the first time we're giving you on memo. I've seen you before but I don't remember what about. — Are you in the jewelry business? Then you know what you're looking at: what could it be? — *Take this, Jake. Call from Louisiana.* — Max, you still here? Already we lost money on you. — What do you want? I don't have eleven-sixteenths in extra short. Try a materials house. — *Yes, Mr. Matos, but you'll have to take care of the engraving.*

Then the phone rang for Mr. Handy personally. It was Moselle and my heart sank.

"I see you made it, Saul."

172

"Oh, yes. I was about to phone you."

"Your friend Bender is here."

"What the hell for?"

"Diamonds."

"Did you pull the alarm?"

"Nothing like that. His wife is with him – a lovely person."

"Isn't she though! Hold everything, Barney; I'm on my way."

I told Murray Corbin I was going out and might not be back that day.

"This should clear it up," I assured him.

"I hope so on your account." They were a pair, those Corbins.

I washed my hands, which were black from dirt, jeweler's rouge, polishing cloths, ink, and gold dust, and put on my jacket and the sporty topcoat.

Forty-seventh Street was swirling. The whole mob was out: everybody and everything that makes the street. No Bartolomi, though, and I didn't see Schultz. It was 1:30; I should have been hungry. . . .

I walked past two store fronts and into Moselle's Exchange. Lila was standing outside the counters of Moselle's section. Henry and three clerks were inside. At the farthest point, his back to me, Barney waited on two distinguished guests from Crestmere.

Lila was beautiful. She wore a knitted suit of a dark electric blue. A gold choker touched the neckline, a massive turquoise bracelet lay on the white skin of one arm, her belt, of the same material as the dress, had a curious gold buckle that she had probably hammered out herself, and her onyx eyes flashed under black, high hair.

Those eyes were on me. When I walked up to her, she held out her hand.

"How are you, Saul?" she said, the voice almost deep.

"Not too bad, Lila. Barney's waiting for me."

"I can't blame you for hurrying." She inclined her head toward the group. "A gem for you to look at."

"I couldn't afford it."

She raised her eyebrows. I proceeded toward what the well-dressed policy-master carried on his arm that year.

Helene was beautiful. She wore a simple mink stole which fell down and down from her high shoulders. Her superb long neck gave the fur all the accent it needed. When I said, "Hello, Barney," she turned her head like something on a pedestal, and I blinked into purple-blue.

"Good morning, Mrs. Bender."

Not even a bitter look. Her hard-featured husband merely said, "No phone call."

"I was interrupted – a pain in the neck."

His eyes were questions but I turned mine to the little counter pad that lay in front of Moselle. On its black velvet a brilliant beauty - the third of the group - demurely accepted our admiration. The pear-shape was familiar; it looked very much like 5.21 carats.

"This," said Moselle, "is the stone I meant you to show to Mrs. Bender."

I didn't say anything. Bender remarked, "It looks like the other one."

"It's two points lighter," I said, keeping my eyes on Helene, "but the blood makes up for that."

They all jumped a little, Helene perhaps the most.

"If you want it," Moselle said to Bender, "it's yours."

Bender looked at me, at his wife, and at Moselle.

"For how much?"

"I've been paid for it once," Moselle answered gravely. "Do you want me to handle the mounting?"

Now Moselle held the stage: his tall, erect body, his pink skin, his tired gray eyes.

"Thanks, Barney," I said.

Bender studied him. "Any time you're playing poker, Mr. Moselle, I'd feel honored to sit in the game."

"It's lovely," Helene decided.

Only Lila remained silent. True, there was nothing in it for her.

"Mount it up," said Bender. "Saul advised a plain mounting, three prongs, handmade."

"Shall I send it to your office?"

"I can stop for it."

Moselle picked up the unblushing cause of it all and put her in her paper. "I'll need until Thursday," he said. "A handmade mounting takes longer."

"The last delay, Mrs. Bender," I put in as the party started to break up. "I always carry out my obligations - only sometimes I'm a little weak on delivery."

She did smile slightly (hard stones thaw hard women), so I added: "I'll see you at the Raphael D'Arle auction. You and Mrs. Moselle, I imagine."

The two women gave each other eyes which did everything that was possible without a loupe.

"Auction?" said Helene.

"His paintings – his effects. The price will be rising. Raphael is now an old master."

Everybody stared at me; maybe they thought I was working on commission. "I knew you ladies would be interested. - That's life: Al Light goes down; Raphael D'Arle goes up. A victory for the arts."

"Let's go, dear," Bender said quietly. "Fill me in, Saul, as soon as you can."

As soon as they filled in Schultz. Good-by, good-by, charmed, delighted, hissed the women. A segment of New York society receded toward the door, gabardine and mink waving softly.

I turned to Moselle to try to say something adequate, but he said: "I've kept a man sitting in my office for two hours. He wants to unload half the Kimberley mines on me. Why don't you phone me later, Saul, and we'll arrange to get together for dinner tonight? Maybe we'll eat out – I'd like to be brought up to date myself."

"I will, Barney." We shook hands and we meant it. Lila and I watched his back go through the entrance to his office.

I looked around the floor. It was crowded, not a booth without a shopper. Moselle's counter had a few people: Henry was showing diamond watches, three clerks were talking to possible buyers, no one was near us – near that sleek, slender woman and the almost well-dressed salesman who could hardly have been her companion.

"Lila," I said, "could I talk to you?"

"Of course."

"Not here," I felt that I looked hesitant, diffident. "Can you open the workshop? Could we go there for a few minutes?"

She gave me a look that blended wonder and provocation in an odd mixture. "You, too," she said, "settle for what you can get." She picked up her unobtrusive broadtail wrap and we walked out of the glittering exchange for all the world like a couple of shoppers from Katonah looking for an anniversary present.

Into the street and out of the street and the elevator brought us to the fourth floor. Lila took a key out of her clever gold-clasped bag, opened the door, stepped over the trip-cord stitched at knee height along the floor, and gave Holmes the signal that satisfied their insistent ring. I noticed that a Holmes alarm bar ran under her worktable; to set it off all she would need was to push her foot under it.

I followed her in after she unstrung the trips, the door locked behind me, and I sat down in the same chair I had used before. She rested on her bench.

"Say something nice, Saul."

I smiled, still uncertainly, I imagine. "It's not hard to say something nice to a girl like you, Lila."

We were less than two feet apart. The sun shone through the one window. The bench, the table, the sofa, the scales, the little furnace, the lathe, and the row of tools – everything lay, neat and ready, at rest in the artist's studio. The same books peered out of the same corner; the same woman challenged me from the bench – alive, reserved, doubtful.

She leaned forward and put her hand lightly on my knee.

"Say it then, Saul. And do it."

I covered her hand. "What is nice?"

"Don't you know?"

"Maybe. Like what?"

"Like you want to say to Mrs. Bender."

"Would I like to say something nice to Mrs. Bender?"

"Don't tell me you're this way with all the girls."

I pressed her firm, muscular hand. "I've had some rough days since I saw you."

"What's wrong?"

"Somebody hit me."

The hand turned cold and her eyes clouded.

"Where? When? Were you hurt?"

"I was hurt. I've also been some place."

She said nothing; we sat in sunny silence.

"I've been to Muskingdon."

The hand was ice. I realized that I was chilled myself from knees to feet. She withdrew her hand and I went on:

"Raphael D'Arle came from Muskingdon. And Al Light. Two brothers. The brothers Carlo."

Her eyes were spots of light. She said in her deepest tones, "And someone else."

"Someone else. Dufort."

She nodded. "Lila Dufort."

"You must have wanted very badly to forget - that change of name. Not that it got you much forgetfulness."

"It was strange," she said, "very strange. Such a small town, Muskingdon, and yet all the world wasn't big enough to keep it away."

I stirred in an effort to relieve my numbness.

"That was a dreadful story I heard in Muskingdon."

She opened her hands. "Must we?"

"What's the use trying to ignore it? Did it help? Does it ever? Barney doesn't know — not if he thinks you're from Wyoming."

"He doesn't know."

"You told me Missouri to keep away from it."

She seemed puzzled herself. "That wasn't like me."

"Does Bartolomi — ?"

"*No!*" (Too rapidly.)

Unfortunately I don't smoke. Neither did she. It would have been the right time to light cigarettes. I asked, "Do you have any liquor here, Lila?"

She turned around, opened a drawer, and took out a dusty, unopened bottle of Scotch. Rotating it slowly in her exquisite hands, she read the label.

"This has lain here four, five years. A supplier left it for Christmas." She stopped and looked up at me. "I believe it was Schultz. That was the first year I ever used him."

177

"You won't use him again."

A shiver swept her from head to foot. "No. No." She peered into my face, seeking answers. "I won't."

I said, "The women really went for that Raphael, didn't they?"

She seemed surprised. "I guess they did."

"Did your sister, Henriette, love him very much?"

No answer to that one. I got up, took the bottle, washed it in the sink, rinsed a drinking glass, and poured two fingers' worth. "To tragic stories, Lila, and to lovers crossed, wherever they are."

I swallowed the Scotch and started to pace the floor. "Did she love him very much?"

"She was very young."

"Seventeen, wasn't it?"

"That's all."

"You Duforts really are an old jewelry family. French-Swiss?"

"Yes. I was raised over a polishing wheel. I used to say that my first lipstick was jeweler's rouge."

"Raphael was a fine designer, wasn't he?"

"Very."

"Was he a good teacher?"

"The best."

"Did you love him much?"

"Must I answer that?"

"No."

Her eyes left mine and went down to her alligator shoes. "I must have."

I poured more whisky. "The tragedy was remarkable, Lila, not only for its senselessness, but for the poor quality of the police work."

"Police . . . ?"

"I used to be a policeman, as you have often mentioned." (I don't know why I felt apologetic about it.) "I can't help noticing certain things. It was only a local investigation. They didn't even do the obvious."

"There was . . . fingerprint business. And medical examination."

"Which showed nothing. Henriette hadn't been raped.

178

She wasn't pregnant. She was still a virgin, in fact. There was no reason to suspect her boy friends."

"She only had one. His time was accounted for."

"Accounted for. Then, for then. Now, forever."

Another tremor went over her, a deep wavering shiver. I felt unsteady myself; my neck seemed to be throbbing and I felt the dull push of a headache.

Lila said, "Why are we talking this way?"

"I've been hurt, Lila. Hit hard. Someone tried to kill me or didn't care if they killed me. It makes a man wonder. For instance, was Al Light's time accounted for?"

"Albert? He had nothing to do with Henriette."

"Nor with the killing in my car. Nor with his brother. Brothers do kill brothers but not this time. He didn't kill Schultz either. It's just that he was such a bad one."

"Not in those days. I wouldn't say so then. He was the high school football hero."

I let my tongue touch the whisky. "People out there have wondered. After the rumors came in. They came to believe that Alberto might have done anything."

"He might have, later. He became a terrible man."

"How would you know?"

"Roberto – Raphael told me."

"Did Bartolomi?"

"No! Not Battista."

"Who found you first in New York?"

"Raphael. So strange. So natural. I went to an art show. Battista gave me the ticket. The first picture threw me way off . . . I seemed to hear something. The second was just as queer. But it was the third one that took me home. I knew that one! And when I turned around I knew the painter."

"And?"

"That was it. That was as far as I had got by leaving home."

"And Raphael told Light?"

"He must have. Within the year. We never discussed it. Raphael had a horror of his brother. They seldom saw each other. Maybe Albert saw us together."

179

I went close to her and put one arm around her shoulders, drawing her against me.

"Were you lovers, Lila? You and Raphael? Here in New York perhaps?"

I couldn't see her face. "No. You might have expected that. But never. Never in Muskingdon. Never here while I was single. Never since I married . . . I wasn't his type."

"Strange."

"Why? I don't seem to be the type for many men."

I raised my free hand from her shoulder to her cheek and bending, kissed her mouth. "You're my type."

She turned her head to look at me under those raised eyebrows. I went on. "I know that D'Arle wasn't the kind to throw anything over his shoulder; I know that much about him."

"Only me. I went over his shoulder."

"Do you think that the memory of Henriette stopped him?"

She trembled again; I could feel it run along my body. "Who knows? Memories! . . . Memories! Memories are hell. Hell stood between us."

I let go of her and sat down. "What bothers me, Lila, is the murder weapon."

"What murder weapon?"

"The blunt instrument. The club, tire iron, whatever it was. They never found it."

"Is that unusual?"

"Yes, if Henriette was killed by an intruder. A stranger. Why would a stranger take the murder weapon away? In broad daylight? He would drop it where it fell. Blunt instruments are usually found except in one case."

I took her hand, put it on my knee again, and laid mine over it.

"The murder weapon is found ordinarily except in a family killing where it is some simple household tool which can be washed off, if necessary, put back in its place, and never be suspected. Only an exhaustive investigation by a large police organization would find that – after lab tests on every conceivable object. What bothers me, Lila, is that they didn't check the first object any jewelry man would have suspected in a house full of jewelers."

Her eyes were points of light again and the hand wasn't warm under mine.

"What?"

"A ring mandril. A common, twelve-inch, tapered, well-balanced, hard steel ring mandril. A tool whose very shape suggests a club. The natural weapon in a jewelry workshop."

"Henriette," she said with difficulty, "was killed in her own bedroom."

"And the shop was all the way back in the barn. No intruder would first go to the shop and get a mandril. Only a member of the family would do that."

"But why a mandril? What reason is there to suspect a mandril? Do we blame the mandril because we blame the family and blame the family because we blame the mandril?"

"No. I blame the mandril because the mandril suggests to me another weapon. The mandril suggests something else, something of much the same shape, of the same murderous usefulness, and the other thing dances before my eyes, Lila. I see it in my dreams. – A mandril isn't so good. A mandril may have ring-size markings which the murderer mustn't take off if he doesn't want explanations. All he can do with a mandril is wash it and scrub it and try to take the blood off. But not that other thing. *That* he can put in a kiln and burn it, and put it on a lathe and polish it, and no water, no impotent, ineffective water need touch it.

"And the family. There are three motives for murder in every family: hate, greed, jealousy. What family ever had no hate? What family ever had no greed? And if we ignore these two, what family ever had no jealousy?

"That's what those village constables should have looked for, jealousy. Two sisters, one man – jealousy. And then a weapon that would suit a jeweler, a weapon that would lead a jeweler on to a better one, to a perfect one."

I took a breath, gulped my whisky, gripped her stone-dead hand, and said:

181

"The weapon that killed Al Light. The weapon that killed Raphael D'Arle. The weapon that killed Schultz!"

We stared into each other's eyes. I was crushing her knuckles with all my force but she didn't feel it.

"Alberto Carlo, Lila: Al Light. One blow and me left with the corpse.

"Brother Roberto – that was quick: my arms at seven and his life at ten. Would you have killed Raphael if I had got down on the floor with you, Lila? Would that have saved him? Would that have made you feel safe?

"Schultz – he guessed something. Probably nothing worth knowing . . .

"On that landing – *did I know?* Did you know whom you were hitting when you held your breath in that hallway? When you raised the thing that was better than a mandril? When you swung the thing?"

I let go of her hand: Mine was paralyzed. Our faces were set each on the other as if we had died that way and her pupils had spread until I could see in the holes. Now I raised my hand and pointed at her bench.

"Did you mean to kill me when you swung it – swung *that thing there?*"

She turned her head and looked where I pointed: at the platinum tube which should have been in the safe but now lay like a sausage along her bench.

She snapped. The hand I had held went around to the bench, she seized the massive length of metal with the grasp of a tennis player, the precious bringer of death started on its sinister arc–

"Another one, Lila?"

She shortened the swing, shortened and weakened it. I leaned back slightly and my hand brushed hers softly along the curve. The platinum passed before my eyes, the swing speeded up a little, it reached her shoulder, and she let it go when the arm came to rest across her chest.

The tube sailed the rest of its short, stolid path and banged dully on the floor – a stupid sound. Her right hand clutched her left breast as if she had been shot.

I stood up. She rose after me.

"Time to stop, Lila." I patted her cheek. The Holmes

bar caught my eye and I added, "You could push your foot under that alarm and say I tried to kill you."

She gave me a level glance, as calm as on the day I had first seen her: "I don't do anything cheap." Her eyes closed for a minute and she added, "Besides, I'm tired."

The hand that had guided the platinum through five deadly courses picked up the telephone and she said, almost immediately:

"Mr. Moselle, please."

A moment later: "Barney. Come up to the studio. . . . I know, dear, but this is more important. Or so you will think. Mr. Handy has completed his case. The matter is concluded. All over. . . . All over. He has only to arrest a murderess."

XXVI

The White Lily at night, with the bright, sad lights on the dirty decorations, and the sad, drab customers seated about the dirty floor, is no place to wash down four murders, not to speak of a friend ruined, one's love destroyed, and the ache of a brutal assault. I could find better places; better places rotted gaily all over town, but I still had one inquiry to make.

I looked at the bartender across my glass. He was a bulky Greek, pockmarked, and his face suggested that he might slaughter his family if he ever went home.

"George," I asked, "what's with Rose?"

It was Saturday, thirty hours since Mrs. Bernard Moselle had phoned for her husband and three and one-half days since Rose had been released by homicide. I hadn't seen Rose since the night of her arrest.

George said, "She's working."

"Is she bad?"

"What can you expect? She's beat."

"Can she do her work?"

"She's drinking. In the morning. Ten, twelve beers."

"She never used to, did she?"

"Not here, for sure."

I went outside. Ten, twelve beers. In the morning. I couldn't stop that. I hadn't wanted to find her damn Bud in the first place. Bud hadn't been so good for her, or for Lila either.

There wasn't a thing I could do. The first time I sat at her table she would stop her pained eyes from turning away and within a week either I would be eating in the Blarney Stone or she would have quit.

184

After she quit? Skid row?

I went back into the avenue. It was busy now with a different kind of life; Forty-seventh Street was dark and still. Dull caverns of black replaced the glittering windows of the day. The girders of new construction loomed stark over the street; there would be new lofts, new exchanges, new memos, new diamonds, new enameled women, and new tired men.

My eyes and my mind fastened on one spot: Moselle's Exchange. The big man who owned it was a half-dead man now. Everything was ruined: wife, life, business most likely, and him too old to start again. Like Rose, he would have been better off if he hadn't asked me to look into things. True, I had solved his problem. No more ominous pear-shapes would creep into his stock. No sleek, gem-hard, all-accomplished pear-shapes would creep into his bed either.

Lila's story had been simple enough once she told it, and she had told it with the same firmness that had guided her tools to beauty and to death.

She was already resetting pieces for Bartolomi when Light had found her. She claimed she did not know at what time that the stones she set were stolen, which may have been true. Light knew, from the underworld, that Bartolomi was an outlet. Bender of course was outside all this; his operations were of another order.

Light did not make his move until Lila married Moselle. That opened a magnificent market, and Light, who seems to have done a little trading in hot goods as a side line, went to Bartolomi. He knew, pretty nearly, who had killed Henriette; moreover, Lila had reset stolen goods, knowingly or not. The two criminals decided to put on the screws.

She claimed, both to Cassidy and to the district attorney, that she fought them down the line. She claimed she had tried to protect her husband. She also showed throughout a strange loyalty toward Bartolomi. She had not fed more than *two hundred thousand* dollars' worth of stolen diamonds into her husband's stock when I turned up. Unfortunately, the Israeli diamond was part of it.

It was too much for her: Marder, her husband, me, that stone, and Light's name in Marder's mouth. When she

185

heard I had been a detective and realized that I would try to solve the case in self-defense, it broke her. She resolved to find a way out.

The way was as simple as her story. She went into the parking lot to get her car and her terrible past ruled her soul so completely that she had already gone to her studio and put the tube of platinum into her bag. When she spotted Al Light in my car all she had to do was remember Henriette. Unfortunately Light didn't. She joined him in the back seat; they had a few bitter words; he saw me coming into the lot, and he never saw again. She left him where he lay; she wasn't ten feet from me when I got into my car. A burr on the platinum drew a few drops of her blood.

D'Arle would have lived to dribble and smear his life away if Lila had not gone to Quinones' party. She heard me ask for Raphael and by the name of Robert Karl. Clearly I was on the trail: Robert Karl, Roberto Carlo, Al Light, Muskingdon, Henriette-

She rushed over to D'Arle's studio. Raphael suspected she had killed his brother just as he had suspected she had killed his sweetheart. They had a nice talk, running with blood, which left him still in some doubt (I *might* have done it) and left her in no doubt. I did call on Raphael, who couldn't make up his mind how to play it, but of course preferred to keep out if possible, and then she called on Raphael. After he told her everything I had said, she went home and I presume she thought about mandrils and tubes for two days.

My love-making was not very promising. She visited Raphael once more and this time her handbag was weighted.

Schultz was inevitable. She hit him when he turned his back to lead her into the inner office. (He probably knew nothing except that Light and D'Arle were brothers). I came too soon for my appointment and she did what she felt she had to do. She couldn't honestly decide whether she had tried to kill me or not. Her last words to me were:

"At bottom I'm truthful, Saul. I meant whatever I said to you and I have never told you a lie."

186

She said this in front of her husband, which did no harm; he was far beyond such subtleties.

Moselle stood by her like a rock but a shattered one. He would get the best lawyers and they would put on a brilliant defense, after which, later, she would be put to death. Unless they pleaded insanity. – A jury, seeing her in emeralds and gold, might well believe that she couldn't possibly have done such things in her right mind.

I wondered whether Helene Bender would get her diamond in time.

So I stood on the avenue. It hadn't much for me. It should have had. I was single, only thirty-four, with a new car, no responsibilities, $2,000 in the bank, and a half-interest in the family burying plot in Springfield. The world lay in front of me, but all I could see was Moselle's Exchange.

It was seven o'clock. I was very tired; it was time to go home; a destination I had failed to provide. I couldn't think of a thing to do or a friend to look for. I might have had a friend, Moselle, or I might have had a love – she said she was truthful – but it hadn't worked out.

I've mentioned that the Corbins had a baby sister, a quiet, friendly, single girl, under thirty. I had spoken to her a few times in the store. I turned back into the White Lily, got her on the phone, and we made a date for the same evening. What was there for me, the way I was going?